CANDLELIGHT
Ecstasy Supreme

"I'M SORRY, JO. I SHOULD NEVER HAVE KISSED YOU." CHASE PUSHED HER AWAY GENTLY.

"Why?" She blinked in an attempt to clear her head. Why on earth was he apologizing?

"It was a thoughtless thing for me to do. For a moment I forgot."

"I don't understand," she murmured in confusion.

"Don't understand? You're pregnant!" he reminded her angrily, turning away.

Jo lowered her head. "I know that. But I still have feelings, Chase. I enjoyed that kiss. From the way your heart was pounding, I think you did too."

"I'm sorry, Jo." He shook his head. "But we both know it's wrong."

CANDLELIGHT ECSTASY SUPREMES

JUST FOR THE ASKING

Eleanor Woods

A CANDLELIGHT ECSTASY SUPREME

Published by
Dell Publishing Co., Inc.
1 Dag Hammarskjold Plaza
New York, New York 10017

Dell ® TM 681510, Dell Publishing Co., Inc.

Candlelight Ecstasy Supreme is a trademark
of Dell Publishing Co., Inc.

Candlelight Ecstasy Romance®, 1,203,540, is a
registered trademark of Dell Publishing Co., Inc.

ISBN: 0-440-14405-1

Printed in the United States of America

First printing—September 1985

To Our Readers:

Candlelight Ecstasy is delighted to announce the start of a brand-new series—Ecstasy Supremes! Now you can enjoy a romance series unlike all the others—longer and more exciting, filled with more passion, adventure, and intrigue—the stories you've been waiting for.

In months to come we look forward to presenting books by many of your favorite authors and the very finest work from new authors of romantic fiction as well. As always, we are striving to present the unique, absorbing love stories that you enjoy most—the very best love has to offer.

Breathtaking and unforgettable, Ecstasy Supremes will follow in the great romantic tradition you've come to expect *only* from Candlelight Ecstasy.

Your suggestions and comments are always welcome. Please let us hear from you.

Sincerely,

The Editors
Candlelight Romances
1 Dag Hammarskjold Plaza
New York, New York 10017

CHAPTER ONE

The tall, tanned man, his light-brown hair streaked by the sun, entered the small lobby of the hotel, if the rickety one-and-a-half-story building could be called such. His long stride quickly covered the short distance to the front desk. He reached over the waist-high structure and picked up a mail pouch. He then turned and walked into another larger room that doubled as a gathering place for the locals in the evenings and a restaurant during the day.

Two children, a boy and a girl, were in the room cleaning vegetables for the next day's fare. They eyed the tall American with a mixture of shyness and expectancy. There was no understanding the gentle giant's ways, they had decided, but if they were around each afternoon when he came back from the huge "wall of concrete and dirt" he was building just north of their village, he would usually give them a few coins for the small chores they performed for him. The ritual rarely varied. This day was no exception.

The man made his way to the same table by the window he'd sat at each evening since his arrival in the tiny Central American village. He gave a brief nod to the boy watching him, and in minutes a bottle of scotch and a glass were placed before him.

The boy watched as the man withdrew a number of coins from his pants pocket and placed them on the table. "Thank you, Fernando." The man spoke in a deep voice. "Be sure and give something to your sister."

Fernando smiled, grabbed the money, and scooted back to the worktable where his sister was watching.

Chase Colbern bit at his sensuous bottom lip as his cobalt-blue eyes watched the youngsters. Damn! but he missed his son Bink. He removed the cap from the scotch bottle and poured a generous amount into the glass. Then he reached for the mail pouch. Again his hand went to his pants pocket and pulled out a small key. After opening the pouch, Chase returned the key to his pocket.

He had a feeling there would be a letter for him from his son. During the last year or so, Bink had taken to writing letters as if he'd just discovered that particular means of communication. Chase poured the contents of the pouch onto the table, except for one white envelope, which he set aside. This letter had lent its aromatic fragrance to the inside of the pouch and all the other letters. Chase twitched his nose distastefully. Where the hell did Alex find that damned perfumed stationery?

With a quick hand he flipped through the mail, a look of pleasure softening the leathery harshness of his features when he spotted the letter he was searching for.

He settled back, hooking the tip of his heavy work boot between the two bottom rungs of a nearby chair. After a healthy sip of scotch, he opened the letter.

May 1

Dear Dad,

I sure do miss you. I'm broke. Jake grounded me for a week. My baseball accidentally broke the new neighbor's window. The neighbor didn't get mad, but Jake sure cussed a blue streak. I have to mow our yard and the neighbor's too, as punishment. I got a base hit and a single in last night's game. Wish you could've been there.

Love,
Bink

Chase read the letter over and over, wondering as he did what in the hell he was doing working on a dam in some godforsaken place when his kid was growing up without him. It was a question he'd been asking himself for several months now.

Lately the quest for freedom he'd always sought so eagerly hadn't seemed as important as it had been, say, a year ago. The open spaces and the one-on-one with nature weren't as enticing as they had been in years past.

Chase put the letter back into the envelope, then stared broodingly into the amber liquid in his glass. God! He was nearly forty. He felt old and tired. The way of life he'd thought he couldn't live without had become nothing more than a daily drudge.

Oh, the thrill of seeing his work go from a series of blueprints to a real construction before his very eyes was exciting. He was an engineer, and a damned good one. The fact that he could design and oversee the erection of a hydroelectric dam in a Third World country was exhilarating. The challenge of building a bridge over an otherwise impassable gorge brought a surge of excitement to him. But lately it wasn't enough. Not nearly enough.

Even the exciting bachelor life had lost some of its appeal. When he found himself sitting across the table from a gorgeous redhead, wondering why the hell he was bored, he knew he had a problem.

Pushing his unpleasant thoughts aside, Chase finished going through the mail. Finally only the perfumed letter remained. He opened it, his face expressionless as he read.

To anyone happening to catch sight of the single sheet of paper with a gaudy rose embossed on the corner, it would look as if Chase were involved in a steamy affair with a very sexy lady named Alex. It was supposed to look that way, Chase thought with a grin. But between paper and pen and actuality, he quietly mused, it became a different story.

He downed the rest of the scotch, poured another, then returned all the mail, except Bink's letter, to the pouch. So Alex had another job for him. And from the way it sounded, his assignment to deliver a "parcel" to the States would coincide perfectly with the completion of the dam.

May 6

Dear Dad,

I traded Joey that old fishing reel of yours for a really neat skateboard. Hope you don't mind. Jo, that's our new neighbor, got a new motor scooter today. I went for a ride on it and Jake got mad at me. I miss you.

Love and broke,
Bink

Chase was lying on the narrow bed in his room, his eyes greedily absorbing each word his son had written. Who the hell was this Jo character? Didn't he know that kids Bink's age had no business riding damn motor scooters? Chase sat up, reached for a yellow legal-sized pad of paper, and began scribbling. Jake must be getting old to have let something like that happen.

Dear Dad,

Thanks for the money. I bought a new tape by the Dirt Bags. They're real neat. Jake says they ought to have their "you-know-what's" kicked, but I caught him humming along during one of the songs. I had to go over and feed Jo's cat. It's a weird cat, it's almost as mean as Jake, but Jo is neat. Even Jake likes Jo. Well, I've got to go, the *A-Team* is about to come on. I hit a home run last night.

Love,
Bink

Chase frowned. This damn Jo person seemed to be taking up a lot of Bink's time. Well, Chase would be home in a few weeks, and his new neighbor could darn well find another kid to lavish affection on. Bink had a father.

There was also a letter from Jake in the pouch that day. An ex-military man and "keeper" of the Colbern hearth and home, Jake informed his employer that if he didn't care for the way his son was being raised, he could damn well get his rear end back home and do the job himself. As for their neighbor, Jake further stated, it was a sad day indeed when Chase Colbern resented a little human kindness being shown his son by a very nice person. A sad day indeed!

First Bink and now Jake had taken to this neighbor, Chase thought grimly. The list of transgressions committed by "neighbor Jo" were steadily mounting. A man's home and family were sacred, and this fellow was definitely intruding.

May 19

Dear Dad,
    Jake invited Jo to eat dinner with us last night. Jake fixed roast beef. We lost our last two games. Sorry, but I've got to go now, Jo is taking me to a movie.

Love,
Bink

Chase was fuming. He was thousands of miles from home and his position as Bink's father was being undermined by a jackass named Jo. Jo! he thought scathingly. Why the hell was a man spelling his name that way, anyway? That alone was enough to make Chase have serious reservations about the fellow as a role model in his son's life.

Another letter from Alex placed Chase's parental concern on hold. The "parcel" he was to be in charge of would be waiting for him in Puerto Cortes, a city on the northern coast of Honduras. Information concerning tentative times, dates, and transportation—a boat, then a seaplane near the Bay Islands—was included. More precise instructions would follow.

Chase stared thoughtfully into the flickering glow of the lamp that provided the only light in his room. From the coded messages in Alex's letters he knew the "parcel" was a defector from a communist country, and an important one at that. An unexpected shiver of apprehension ran through him.

Since becoming a government agent ten years before, Chase had always found the risk exciting . . . until now. He'd had some close shaves once or twice, but had considered it all part of the game. This was the first time, however, when he found himself dreading an assignment. And that, my friend, is when you know it's time to get out, he told himself.

The freedom with which he could travel all over the world as an engineer was a perfect cover for an agent. When he'd been approached by Alex Grenwyck ten years ago, Chase hadn't hesitated. Over the years a firm friendship had developed between the two men. Chase's assignments were carefully chosen to take into consideration two important factors. One was Bink. The other was the risk to the Colbern Engineering Company in the different countries where his work as an agent was carried out. Few, if any, governments would willingly allow an agent for the United States government to roam at will throughout their country. If Chase's cover were blown, it would mean financial disaster for his family's firm.

If Chase's father and his two brothers in the home office in Houston ever suspected that he was involved in any activity other than Colbern Engineering, they never let on. Chase had always gone his separate way and they respected his privacy. Wouldn't they be surprised, Chase thought with amusement, when he arrived home in a few weeks to announce that he was through traveling? His mother would probably kill the fatted calf.

May 24

Dear Dad,
    Sorry I haven't written sooner, but our team made the playoffs. We lost in the second game though. Grandma, Grandpa, Uncle Brent, Jake, and Jo came to see me play. I wish you could have been there. Jo says it was terrible for you not to get to see me. Jo's real neat, Dad. I hope you two will like each other. Jo said it would be nice if you could get a job closer to home. Do you think you could? If you can't, send me some money.

Love,
Bink

Chase read the letter through twice, angrily gritting his teeth, then began throwing his clothes in a bag. His hands itched to clamp themselves around the saintly Jo's neck. Closer to home indeed! Well, he was going to be closer to home, he thought, smiling savagely, and in only a few hours at that. He could hardly wait to tell his meddling neighbor exactly where to go.

He quickly glanced at his watch, his mind already on the itinerary Alex had sent him. There would be a long, hard ride to Juticalpa. From there he would be flown to Puerto Cortes by private plane, with "Colbern Engineering" plastered on the side in large, clear letters for appearances' sake. If things went according to plan, he would meet Alex, take possession of the "parcel", go by boat to the Bay Islands, board another plane, and fly home to Houston.

Chase walked into the hotel in Puerto Cortes with his heavy leather travel bag slung over his shoulder and carrying a briefcase. His blue eyes quickly scanned the lobby for Alex. Not seeing him, Chase checked his bags with the desk clerk, then found his way to the bar.

It took a few seconds for his eyes to adjust to the dimness of the room. Still not spotting Alex, Chase chose a table where he could keep a watchful eye on the door. He ordered a drink and then sat down to wait. He'd learned, during his years as an agent, that patience was a prerequisite to working in that particular profession.

It was only just after six o'clock, and already business was beginning to pick up in the bar. Chase sat sprawled in his chair, one hand loosely clasping his glass as he watched the patrons, all of them eager for a night of fun.

He must have waited nearly an hour when suddenly, out of the corner of his eye, he saw Alex enter the bar. He didn't come through the door Chase had been watching, but through a curtain at the right.

Alex made his way through the steadily growing crowd to where Chase was sitting and slipped into the vacant chair at the small table. "And how was your day?" He grinned as they shook hands. Fatigue was etched in his features, and his clothes looked as though he'd been wearing them for more than one day.

"I've had better." Chase sat forward, his alert gaze taking in his friend's rumpled condition. "You don't look as though you've faired too well. Trouble?"

He shrugged. "You could say that. There are those who would like to see this little excursion aborted."

"I expected as much," Chase murmured. "Let me get you a drink, then fill me in on what's happened." He went to the bar, got the drinks, and returned. "So," he began as he sat back down, "tell me about it."

"We lost an agent three days ago. Guy by the name of Rascom. I don't think you know him, but he's a hell of a good agent. We don't know if he's dead or captured. But"—Alex rubbed his chin with his hand—"you know the rules in our particular group. After thirty-six hours you're crossed off. Your section is closed and all codes erased."

"But you aren't going by the rules, are you?"

Chase asked quietly. He knew Alex Grenwyck. If Alex thought there was a chance in hell of rescuing Rascom, he would take it. "Are you alone or is someone helping you?"

"I've got help. Not the sort I'd like, but double agents do come in handy at times." He took a sip of his drink. "How about you, Chase? Are the vibrations I've been getting from you lately what I think they are? Are you ready to get out?"

"It's that obvious, hmmm?" Chase grinned.

"To someone who feels the same way, I suppose it is," Alex confessed. "I'm tired of trotting around the world playing spy. There's something missing."

"Maybe it's a wife and kids that you need," Chase suggested. He swirled the contents of his glass around and slowly shook his head. "I know I miss my son. Hell, Alex, I'm nearly forty. I haven't been home for more than a month at a time since he was born. He's twelve years old, and I think I've missed about every important event in his life."

"Then get the hell out of this mess and go home. But don't lock the door, 'cause I've got a feeling I won't be far behind you. Houston sounds like as good a place as any for a guy to settle down." Alex took another sip of his drink, then leaned farther over the table. "There's a sweet-looking old lady waiting for you in the lobby. She'll be going with you as far as Hobby Airport in Houston. There

18

will be less confusion at the smaller airport, making it easier for 'Aunt Martha' to be reunited with her loved ones." He told Chase the name of the small boat that would be waiting at a specific location in the harbor for him and Aunt Martha at eight-thirty.

"May I ask exactly who it is I'm risking my life for?"

Alex named a scientist from one of the communist-bloc countries. The identity of the defector brought a low whistle of surprise from Chase. "I certainly hope you've managed to get this far without a host of trigger-happy idiots following you," he said with a scowl.

"Er . . . well, not exactly." Alex grinned sheepishly. "One or two of our neighbors have taken exception to our auntie's trip."

"Which accounts for your sneaking in the back door, hmmm?"

"Precisely."

"Then how the hell am I supposed to get 'Aunt Martha' out of here and on that damn boat without picking up a few shots in my ass?" Chase hissed furiously.

"Picky, picky." Alex laughed. "As of yet, they don't suspect you're involved. Your traveling companion assumed the Aunt Martha disguise this morning. And I honestly think it's worked. When it's time for you to leave the hotel, there will be a suitable diversion. Does that satisfy you?"

It did. And at approximately eight-twenty, a mysterious explosion ripped through an abandoned warehouse a block from the hotel. The noise sent the patrons of the restaurant and bar scurrying out onto the street. No one paid the slightest attention as the tall, tanned American quickly ushered the short, plump figure of the "old woman" from the lobby and down an alley.

God! It was so good to be home, Chase thought as he leaned back in the taxi and watched the familiar landmarks flash by. He took a deep breath of clean Texas air into his lungs and let it out slowly. In a few minutes he would be home with Bink. Seeing his son and being with him had become paramount in his mind. He was determined that he no longer would be a part-time father.

When they turned onto the quiet, treelined street, a quickening of excitement raced through Chase. His home was at the end of the circular cul-de-sac. Rather than turn into the driveway, he directed the driver to park at the curb.

In minutes, Chase was standing beside the taxi, his bags on the edge of the lawn as he paid the driver. The young man gave him a thumbs-up gesture at the nice tip, then gunned the engine of the taxi and pulled away from the curb. Chase turned and was in a bent position as he reached for his luggage. Suddenly the air was filled with the screeching of brakes, the rough sound of the taxi's engine, and a peculiar whirring noise.

Before he could assimilate all these noises, Chase heard a voice shriek, "Look out!" He then felt a tremendous jolt to his rear end and a sharp pain in his right ankle. The next second he was flying through the air like a football. He landed on the front lawn several feet from his bags, a loud *swoosh* of air escaping him. Before he had a chance to gather his shocked and scattered wits, he was again attacked from the rear. This time the object was far softer and landed smack on the middle of his back!

The first coherent thought that entered Chase's befuddled mind was that he had been followed from the airport and that *someone* was more than a little upset with Aunt Martha's decision to vacate her homeland. He screwed his head around, fully expecting to see a gun looking him in the face. What he saw, however, was a pair of startled gray eyes, fringed by thick, dark lashes. Coal-black hair framed a heart-shaped face, with skin as smooth and creamy as a magnolia blossom. A small, turned-up nose and soft pink lips completed the face.

Chase stared at the very attractive, very feminine apparition for a full sixty seconds before he could speak. By then the frightened taxi driver was standing over the fallen pair, his face stricken with horror as he imagined all sorts of lawsuits and injuries.

"I'm sorry, ma'am," the young man began, twisting his cap in nervous hands. "I can't figure it out! One minute the street was clear, the next, you and your motor scooter appeared as if by magic!"

"Well, it damn sure wasn't magic that hit me in the behind," Chase bellowed, as the paralysis gripping his throat disappeared. "Are you hurt?" he asked the woman.

"No . . . no, I'm fine. But I'm so sorry," the small figure sitting on his back offered in a shaken voice. "Do you think you have any broken bones, Mr. Colbern?" she asked tentatively.

"Well, now," Chase replied sarcastically, "just how the hell am I to know with you straddling my back, madam? And how do you know my name?"

"Oh!" The young woman blushed furiously. She scrambled off his backside to her feet, ably assisted in her bumbling efforts by a strong hand from the taxi driver. "You *are* Bink's father, aren't you?"

Chase rolled onto his back, then sat up. "I am," he snapped. "And just who the hell are you?" he asked suspiciously.

"I—I'm Jo. Jo Benoit, your new neighbor."

CHAPTER TWO

Whatever Chase was about to say was effectively cut off by the sound of the front door of a sprawling white house swinging open with a bang. Both Bink and Jake were attempting to rush through the opening at the same time. Bink won and came tearing down the brick-paved walk, a huge grin plastered on his face.

"Dad!" he yelled excitedly, not slowing down until he was on the ground beside his father, his arms around Chase's neck. "Boy!" he exclaimed in an exuberant voice as he drew back. "This is some surprise."

"Hello, Bink!" Chase grinned. One hand snaked out and ruffled the shaggy head. "You've grown at least a foot since I was last home."

"Aw, you're just kidding me." Bink grinned in embarrassment, secretly pleased. He sat back on his heels, his curious gaze sweeping over the scooter leaning against the curb, his father on the ground, and a thoroughly shaken Jo standing next to the taxi driver. "Geez," he said in an awed voice. "What happened?"

"I . . . overshot the driveway again." Jo spoke in an apologetic voice. "When I decided to cut through the alley I had to swerve to avoid hitting a dog. Unfortunately, I lost control of the scooter and almost collided with the taxi."

"The taxi was lucky, it could get out of her way," Chase remarked dryly to no one in particular. "And since my rear end doesn't possess radar, I was a sure-fire target."

"What a happy family reunion," Jake intoned gruffly. He took his time looking over the situation, accepting Chase's abrupt entrance into their lives without the slightest flicker of an eyelash. "Are you all right, Jo?"

"I'm fine, Jake, thank you." She smiled so sweetly, Chase thought he would be sick.

So this was Jo, Chase thought, more than a little surprised. He looked her over closely. Why the hell had Bink led him to believe that "Jo" was a man? Well, it really didn't matter. Still, he'd be sure to make it plain to this . . . this person that Bink wasn't in need of a mother. He sure as hell didn't want his life cluttered up with some screwy woman targeting his son as the recipient of her motherly frustrations.

"Do you plan on sitting on the front lawn for the rest of the day, Chase?" Jake asked.

"No, I hadn't actually planned on it, but since my right ankle is hurting like hell, the idea becomes more appealing by the moment."

"Oh, dear," Jo murmured, horrified. She stepped forward, then went down on her knees. As she did so, she slipped and reached out for support. Her hand landed directly on Chase's injured ankle.

He let forth with a string of oaths that turned the air blue. The taxi driver, after a pitying glance at the startled Jo, turned and made a dash for his taxi. Bink looked from his dad to Jo, never more uncomfortable in his entire life. Even Jake had the grace to glance upward as though searching for some strange and mystic revelation in the heavens.

"Miss Benoit." Chase spoke in cool, clipped tones as soon as he had himself under control. "Will you please get away from me? In less than five minutes since my arrival home, I have been run down by a motor scooter, my backside is aching like hell, and I'm quite positive my ankle is broken."

Jo threw Jake and Bink a nervous smile, looked thoughtfully at Chase, then did as he asked. She walked to the curb where the taxi driver had kindly set the scooter upright for her. After starting the electric engine, she sat for a moment longer, staring at the trio on the lawn. "Er—have a nice day," she offered lamely. Then she carefully steered the scooter a few feet to the next driveway, turned in, and disappeared into the garage at the rear of the house.

Jo leaned against the edge of the counter, remembering the embarrassing scene that had taken place earlier on the Colbern lawn, while she waited for her water to boil for a cup of tea.

She'd known the huge, rugged-looking man was Chase Colbern as soon as she'd seen him. Bink had filled her ears for weeks with stories of his father and had shown her pictures as well. She knew that Chase preferred scotch, that one of his favorite dishes was pot roast, that he was deathly afraid of the dentist, and that he seemed to always have a girlfriend—at least Bink made it sound that way, judging from the number of women he'd mentioned in the course of their many conversations.

From all the information she'd been blessed with regarding her scowling neighbor, Jo couldn't help but wonder if being a father was one of the things Chase disliked most. His long absences from home certainly pointed in that direction. She was well aware that the life of an engineer was hectic. But couldn't he see that Bink needed him?

She sighed as she picked up the hissing tea kettle and poured the steaming water into her mug. Bink's situation brought back memories of her own childhood—a childhood that would have been terribly lonely if she hadn't been born with an imagination that allowed her a perfect escape into a world of make believe.

As she added sugar and lemon to the tea, she thought of her family. Her mother was a lawyer, her father a surgeon. They demanded the same push for excellence in their four children that they channeled into their own lives. One son was a scientist, another a lawyer. One daughter was a stockbroker, while their youngest daughter was— Well, Jo thought, cocking her head to one side, she wasn't exactly sure what she was. An artist with a million and one projects always going on. And while it horrified her overachieving family, her life suited her just fine. She disliked schedules. She disliked having another person regulate her to the point where she felt like a puppet.

She took her mug of tea to the weathered deck that led out from the kitchen and sat down at the glass-topped table. The truth was, she admitted for the hundredth time, she was a bitter disappointment to her family. A soft grin played about her lips as she looked back on how many times she'd changed her major in college. She even found it in her to quietly chuckle at the frustration and anger leveled at her by her parents during those years. They simply couldn't accept that they had created this—this creature without an ounce of drive in her body.

She'd been an avid reader in her youth, assuming the plight of the heroine of each novel she read. Her fruitful imagination had taken some of the sting out of her family's disapproval during her younger years. Her most interesting idea, Jo recalled with a grin as she sipped her tea, was imagining that she was adopted. For months after deciding that she really didn't belong to the people she was living with, she had carefully examined the features of each of her parents' guests, looking for some similarity that would lead her to her *real* family. When that idea became dull, she decided to thwart their efforts to change her into a model child by refusing to bathe. Next had come the ragged clothes period, then the sexy "vamp" stage in her middle teen years.

When her parents pinned her ears back for her shenanigans, she blithely told them that she was trying to "find herself." It took her years to realize that she'd known herself all along. It was her relatives who refused to accept the inevitable.

The sound of the phone ringing roused Jo from her reverie. She got to her feet, catching sight of Chase Colbern and Bink out in the backyard next door. She paused for a moment, watching the way Chase's blue shirt pulled taut across his shoulders as he lifted Bink's bicycle and put it in the trunk of his car. Some hunk, she mused thoughtfully, then turned and hurried into the house.

"Damn it, Jo," Mo Tyson's deep voice boomed into her ear the moment she lifted the receiver. "How do you expect me to make heads or tails of this mess you've scribbled down in the ledger I gave you?"

"Why, Mo," Jo replied with a smile in her voice.

"How nice to hear from you. Can you come over for dinner this evening?"

"Dinner!" he exploded. "How can you talk about food when I'm trying to keep you from going to prison for your preposterous bookkeeping?"

"You really shouldn't get so upset, Mo," she said soothingly. "It isn't good for you. Did you read that article I gave you about stress?"

"No," he barked, though less forceful than a moment ago. "I must have misplaced it." He tried again. "If I bring the ledger with me this evening, will you *please* explain this code you've used in recording your expenditures?"

"Of course, Mo. By the way, how does fried chicken and hot biscuits sound?"

"Delicious." He sighed in defeat. "I'll bring a bottle of scotch."

"That will be nice, Mo. Your last bottle is almost empty. See you around six-thirty." Jo replaced the receiver and reached for her tea. Mo was nice. Somewhat of a bully, but nice.

Knowing she'd played hooky long enough, Jo left the kitchen and headed for what had been the third bedroom, but was now her studio. It was a large room, and she'd nearly gone broke by adding additional windows and two skylights to it. The view from the windows looked out over the Colberns' backyard, which, at the moment, was empty.

The light over the drafting table was still on,

casting into sharp focus the woebegone expression of Thaddeus Frog, a character in the children's book she was illustrating. Jo climbed onto the tall stool, selected a pen, and began to embellish the generous outline of T. Frog's body.

She enjoyed working with the comical figures, and aside from her book-illustrating work, which brought in a large part of her income, she was also one-third owner of a small greeting card company. She did the artwork for the cards, Mary Clare Brent took care of the administrative end, and Carla Channing wrote the verse. It would be some time before there were even moderate profits from their small business venture. But in the meantime, they were able to pay the bills and each draw a small salary. Jo had no doubt that with Mary Clare's sales ability, they would be successful.

Jo had been at work nearly two hours when she heard the sound of voices. She looked up and saw Bink and his father outside playing basketball. Actually, she saw that Bink was doing most of the running around while Chase seemed to stand in one place. As he bent over to retrieve the ball, she could barely make out the Ace bandage wrapped around his ankle. But even with a bum ankle he was one heck of a man, Jo told herself. The frolicking antics of T. Frog forgotten, Jo propped her chin on a fist and watched the man through her window.

Chase was wearing only a pair of faded jeans

and scruffy tennis shoes. But it wasn't what he was wearing that caught Jo's attention, it was the finely toned muscles from his waist up. Her artistic appreciation for nature's handiwork in any form was more than pleased as she watched each movement of his magnificent body while he played with Bink. There were none of the bulging biceps that came from hours of dedicated body building, simply the effortless synchronization of muscle, skin, and bone. And not only had he been blessed with a gorgeous form, there was an air of confidence about him that could only come from within a person. In fact, Chase Colbern was quite possibly the sexiest man she'd ever run into. Even the memory of Lance's dark good looks paled in comparison. Suddenly her pleasant thoughts about her neighbor were interrupted by a loud crash as a basketball met the fragile glass of Jo's window.

At the precise moment of impact, Jo instinctively threw up one arm to shield her face. Fortunately the ball cracked rather than shattered the pane. She lowered her arm and calmly regarded the condition of her window. She saw Bink wave at her, throw a knowing grin at the window, then mischievously regard his scowling father. Chase muttered something to his son and then turned and limped away. A few minutes later Jo heard the front doorbell ring.

On her way to answer, she couldn't help but smile. When Bink had had the misfortune to break one of her windows, Jake had made him mow her lawn. She wondered if Chase had ever had his hands on a lawn mower.

She opened the door to her flinty-eyed neighbor, who looked decidedly annoyed. "Yes?" She smiled pleasantly. Privately she was thinking how much more devastating he was up close. The wiry growth of hair covering his chest was several shades darker than the sun-streaked hair on his head. Without being aware of it, Jo let her curious gaze follow the dark chest hair as it disappeared beneath the low-slung waistband of the jeans.

"I've never had a woman invite me to strip before, but if you're that curious, I'd be happy to oblige, Miss Benoit," Chase smoothly informed her. No wonder Bink was so taken with this damn woman, he thought furiously. Anyone as unorthodox as she appeared to be could capture a young boy's heart in a minute. Thing was, he told himself, she looked so dainty and fragile. And pretty too. Frankly, though, he preferred his women taller. This one was so tiny, you would have to shake the bedclothes to find her.

"As much as I would enjoy sketching you in the nude, Mr. Colbern, I'm afraid I don't have the time today." Jo looked up and met his glowering gaze with her perfectly innocent one. "But I *would* like a raincheck." She stood back. "Won't you come in?"

"Do you do this sort of thing often?" he asked

between clenched teeth as he followed Jo into a surprisingly warm and attractive living room. He had been anticipating something a bit more gaudy, certainly not the early American country decor and the warmth of color that greeted him.

"Do what sort of thing?" Jo asked. She waved him to a seat on the plaid sofa, then sat across from him in a cherry rocker.

"Ask strange men to pose nude for you."

"Actually I've only done it one other time since art school, but it didn't work out," she said frankly.

"What happened?" Chase found himself asking. This had to be the craziest dame he'd ever encountered. There was no way in hell he was going to allow Bink free run of her house.

"I was disappointed once he was undressed," she told him as if they were discussing the weather. "With his clothes on, he looked magnificent. Unfortunately, I soon learned that, on him, clothes covered a multitude of sins. Of course I paid him anyway, so he really didn't lose anything. After that, I stuck with Lance. While he might have been untrustworthy in many ways, at least his body was true. He was also a freebie, which made it even better."

Chase's blood pressure rose to an alarming high and his heart rate accelerated. God! He would kill Jake for trusting this woman! And this Lance character. Who the hell was he? "How lucky for you.

33

Er—what do you usually pay a man to . . . pose for you?"

She named a figure that caused Chase to stare pointedly. "Haven't you heard of inflation?" he quibbled. "That's mere chicken feed these days."

"It's not enough?" Jo looked thoughtful for a moment, her dark head cocked engagingly. "Oh, well, I'll do some checking before we set a date. I certainly wouldn't want to cheat you." She gave him that same sweet, unassuming smile she'd been wearing when she opened the door. "I'm afraid I haven't been a very good hostess. May I offer you a drink? I have wine, bourbon, and scotch."

"Scotch," Chase answered without hesitation, then immediately asked himself why he'd done so. Jo Benoit's morals appeared to be as loose as a sheet flapping in the wind. Worse than that, she made no attempt to hide it. But knowing Bink as he did, Chase would have to have more on the woman before he could convince his son to leave her alone. Bink was very loyal to his friends.

In a moment, Jo was standing before Chase with two drinks. He took the one she handed him, his blue eyes watching every move her petite body made as she walked back to the chair where she'd been sitting. One thing he would have to say for her, he thought fleetingly, she looked damned good in jeans. He couldn't tell much about the rest of her though, because of the baggy shirt she was wearing.

"So," he began uncomfortably, "you're an artist?"

"Well, it's not as glamorous as it sounds, I assure you." Jo shrugged. "I mainly do illustrations for children's books. I'm also part owner of a greeting card company for which I do the artwork. In my spare time I dabble in landscapes, which happen to be a favorite with me. Some I'm lucky enough to sell, others are foisted off on unsuspecting friends. Eventually I'd like to try my hand at portraits." For a man who had broken her window, he certainly was asking a lot of questions, Jo thought. And his concern for the window didn't appear to be on his mind at all. He was a very complex man. He was also full of hostility. She could feel it like an invisible wand being waved over her.

"Would this . . . Lance you mentioned be annoyed if you were to find another model?" Chase's mind had gone into overdrive, conjuring up all sorts of wild orgies he was certain took place regularly. He wasn't a prude, but, damn it, raising a child was difficult enough without a gray-eyed, pint-sized seductress next door.

Jo seemed to hesitate over his question regarding Lance. Finally she shook her head. "Definitely not."

"Very understanding fellow, isn't he?"

"Not really. He's dead."

CHAPTER THREE

Chase had made the fatal mistake of asking the question while raising his glass to his lips. The scotch was making its way down his throat at the same moment he heard the words "He's dead."

Suddenly the scotch was trying to go the wrong way and Chase was wheezing like a giant bellows, his face beet red. Jo sat her glass down on a nearby table and flew to his side, where she began whacking him on the back with all her might.

Dear Lord! Both times she'd met Chase Colbern, something unpleasant had happened to him. "Are you all right?" she cried the moment there was a pause in the coughing and noise coming from her guest.

"Hell yes!" Chase bellowed in a raspy voice, turning watery eyes up to glower at her. "And will you please stop beating me on the back?"

Jo stepped back in embarrassment. Chase Colbern must think her his own personal jinx! "Would you like a glass of water?" she asked quietly. Her palms and fingers were still tingling from the contact with his skin. And for the life of her, she couldn't decide if the sensation came from the blows she'd given him or the smoothness of his warm, tanned back beneath her touch.

"No, thank you," Chase replied hoarsely after taking several deep breaths.

Jo watched him for a few seconds, then walked back to her chair and sat down, her expression unreadable. "I'm sorry if I appeared overzealous in my attempts to help you, but seeing a person choking frightens me."

"Oh?" Chase asked sarcastically. "Was that the cause of your friend Lance's untimely demise?" This woman was irritating as hell, and for some unknown reason he found himself wanting to needle her.

"As a matter of fact, it was. Only he wasn't my friend, he was my husband," she told him matter-of-factly.

This time Chase was careful not to get even a whiff of the scotch. In fact, he carefully set the glass on the table, the look of chagrin and shock on his face strangely at odds with the aura of strength emanating from him. Needling was one thing, but to be a complete ass was something else. He glanced up at Jo and gave a quick shake of his head. "Look," he began awkwardly, "I apologize for that crack. My only excuse is ignorance. Bink never mentioned a husband, so naturally I assumed you were single. In fact, I thought you were a man until this morning."

"It's all right," Jo said softly, and even Chase had to admire the quiet dignity surrounding her.

"Were you with him when it happened?"

"Oh no, he was with his girlfriend. They were sharing an intimate dinner for two when he choked on a piece of roast beef. According to the authorities, she became hysterical and in the interim poor Lance died."

Chase closed his eyes for a moment, his mind reeling from one shock after the other. Without a doubt, this had to be one of the wildest afternoons he'd spent in his entire life. Finally, at a loss, he latched on to the subject that had brought him over in the first place. "I broke your window," he offered almost timidly.

"I know." Jo smiled benignly. "How well do you mow yards?"

Chase blinked. "I beg your pardon?"

"When Bink committed that same 'careless act' —and I'm quoting Jake—his punishment was to mow my yard, plus pay for a new pane of glass."

"Oh—well." Chase smiled with relief. "It's been a long time, but I think I can still handle a lawn mower."

"Good. I was afraid you weren't going to set a good example for Bink. Parents usually go to great lengths instructing their children in what they should and shouldn't do. When the parents make mistakes, though, it's almost always a different story."

"I've always tried to be fair with Bink."

"According to Bink, you're the best father a boy could have."

With easy grace, Chase stood and took an expandable wood ruler from the back pocket of his jeans. "Do you mind if I measure the window? I need to know the size of the piece of glass so that I can replace it."

"Of course," Jo said easily, "let me show you." She swung her feet to the floor and stood. But instead of turning gracefully on her feet and leading the way to her studio, she felt the room do a crazy spin and she would have executed a very poor swan dive if Chase hadn't stepped forward and caught her.

In the midst of the silly spinning world, Jo was vaguely aware of being lifted in strong arms and held against a furry chest that tickled the end of her nose. When the softness of the sofa touched her back, she opened her eyes, her hands clutching at Chase's arms.

"Don't panic, it's all right," he said gruffly. He caught her hands and held them in his warm ones, then sat gingerly on the edge of the sofa. Hells bells! Being around this woman for any length of time could cause a person to have a heart attack. "Have you eaten anything today? And I mean food, not some damn lettuce leaf with cottage cheese on top of it."

"I had bacon and eggs for breakfast and a hamburger and fries for lunch," Jo told him without quibbling. The room was almost back on an even keel, but she was afraid to move for fear of it starting up again. It surprised her that, at the moment, her newest neighbor wasn't being the least bit hostile. Bossy, but definitely not hostile.

"Have you been ill lately? Are you taking any kind of medication that would make you dizzy?"

"No, and that's what puzzles me," she confessed. "This has happened two or three times during the past week. I thought it was some kind of bug and that it would go away."

"Have you considered seeing a doctor?"

"Of course not. I'm not ill."

"Funny," Chase retorted dryly as he crossed his arms across his massive chest and stared down at her disapprovingly. "I could have sworn you damn near fainted a moment ago."

"Point taken," Jo meekly replied.

"If you're new in Houston, then I'm sure my mother can give you the name of a reputable gynecologist."

"Why a gynecologist?" The question came quickly, and for the first time since meeting her, Chase caught the barest hint of agitation in Jo's voice.

He shrugged. "No particular reason, it just

seemed the natural assumption. Would you like me to call my mother?"

"No, thank you." Jo sighed. She pushed herself into a sitting position, lengthening the space between them. "I was born and raised in Houston. I also happen to know a number of competent doctors."

"In that case, I'd suggest you make an appointment with one of them," Chase told her. "You have no business riding that damned scooter while you're feeling this way. You could be killed."

"Thank you," Jo murmured. "I'll take care of it." She attempted to swing her feet to the floor, but decided that unless she wanted her legs dangling across his muscled thighs, she'd best wait. "If you don't mind moving, I'll show you the window."

Chase knew he should do as she asked. It would be the gentlemanly thing, but something held him back. He found his thoughts still lingered on her unexpected reaction to his cute remark about undressing for her, on the fact that she'd been married and was widowed, and on her rather blasé attitude toward her dead husband. Jo Benoit was an enigma, and he was surprised to discover that, disapproving though he was of her, he still wanted to know more about her.

"How long has your husband been dead?" he asked, instead of moving.

Jo wrapped her arms around her drawn up legs

41

and rested her chin on her knees. "About two months. I'd already bought this house and was having it renovated. Our divorce would have been final two weeks after his death. Poor Lance. Not only was he unlucky at cards and women, he didn't fare so well with roast beef either."

Chase remained seated, his brain buzzing. In fact, he wasn't sure he was capable of moving at the moment. The innocent-looking beauty facing him was either the coolest dame he'd ever encountered or the most naive. It would be interesting to find out which she was, he told himself. Only thing was, he wasn't sure he was up to the job.

Later in the day while Chase was replacing the pane of glass in Jo's studio, he found himself glancing curiously about the room. Several canvases were leaning in one corner along with three different easels. There were two file cabinets, a worn leather couch, and another table where she put the finished pages of the various books she worked on. She was talented, he admitted as he looked over the different poses of T. Frog. The fat frog looked as though at any moment it would jump from the pages and hop across the room.

With the last bit of grout in place around the window frame, Chase picked up his tools, then walked over to where the canvases were leaning in one corner of the room. He wondered, as he reached for the first one, if he would see the face of the infamous Lance. But to his surprise, he found himself staring at a sunset so beautiful it was breath-taking. For one incredible moment it seemed as if he'd gone back in time, to the days when he would take off with only a backpack to see the country. To him there had never been anything more beautiful than the sunsets of west Texas and New Mexico. He wondered how his diminutive neighbor had managed to capture such beauty on canvas unless she'd been there.

"I can tell by the expression on your face that you like it." Jo smiled as she came into the room. She'd changed from jeans and baggy shirt to a yellow sundress with spaghetti straps. She had on white sandals and a yellow ribbon held her hair back from her face. She was somewhat relieved to see that Chase had chosen to wear a shirt on this visit as well. It made talking to him much simpler.

"It's beautiful," Chase admitted. "It's also something I never expected to see on canvas."

"I spent a few weeks last summer at a dude ranch in New Mexico. I'm afraid I never got around to riding horses. Most of my time was spent taking pictures and sketching." She walked over and stood by Chase, the top of her head barely reaching the middle of his chest. "You can take that one home with you if you want."

"I like it very much, and I will definitely take it home with me. What are you asking for it?"

"I beg your pardon?"

"Money." Chase frowned. "What price have you put on this particular painting?"

"It's a gift," Jo said easily.

"I'd rather pay for it," Chase continued stubbornly. He didn't want to be under any obligation to this bewitching creature whose perfume was causing him to entertain a number of wild and crazy ideas. Damn! No wonder poor Bink had been hoodwinked. Jo Benoit was pure, raw dynamite to any male from the cradle to the grave!

"I insist. Your accepting the painting will help me feel not quite so foolish for that little escapade I pulled this afternoon. Deal?"

"I'll accept it only on one condition." Chase frowned down at her.

"Yes?"

"You are to go to the doctor first thing in the morning. Deal?"

"Deal." She smiled. "Now, if you aren't in a hurry, why don't you come into the kitchen and talk to me while I cook dinner."

"Do you cook for yourself every meal?" Chase asked curiously, following her out of the room and down the hall. Watch it, you fool, his protective instincts were yelling at him. This one is too close to home, not to mention Bink's involvement with her. Besides, she's such a damn nut, she wouldn't know a real proposition from a man if he hit her in the face with it.

"Not every day, but I'm having company for

44

dinner. Mo has an appetite like a garbage disposal."

"Is Mo a prospective model?" Chase asked, slightly irritated by the thought.

Jo laughed, and the sound was rather a pleasant one to Chase. "When you meet Mo, I think you will have your answer to that question. Now," she said warmly, "why don't you sit over there at the table while I finish fixing dinner? That way we can visit and I'll be able to feed Mo on time."

"I really don't think—"

"Nonsense." Jo smiled, disposing of his refusal with a wave of one hand. "I happen to know that Bink is at a scout meeting and Jake is watching one of his favorite shows on television."

And in less time than he cared to think about, Chase found himself seated at the round oak table in the kitchen. A scotch and water had been set before him without his even asking. His blue eyes followed Jo as she moved from counter to stove in her preparations for dinner. Yes sirree, he mused as he sipped his drink and stared moodily at his hostess. No wonder his whole family was so taken with Ms. Jo Benoit. He'd only known her a few hours, and already he felt as though he'd been run over by a miniature steamroller.

His reaction to Jo, however, was put on hold some forty-five minutes later when her dinner guest arrived. Mo Tyson reminded Chase of a mountain or perhaps a giant redwood. The length and breadth of him seemed to go on forever. Chase found it mindboggling to even try and picture such a person calmly posing nude. In fact, the thought was so comical, it was all he could do to keep from laughing as Jo introduced her guest.

"So you're Bink's dad," Mo boomed as he pumped Chase's hand in a bone-crushing grip. "That's a nice boy you've got there." He took a seat opposite Chase, blithely ignoring the squeaks and groans of the chair. "Are you home for good or is this just a visit?"

"I think for good," Chase easily replied. "Living out of a suitcase isn't as appealing as it once was."

"Yeah." Mo grimaced. "I know what you mean. I worked as an auditor for a large corporation for a number of years. Opening my own accounting firm has been like a constant vacation. With the exception of one or two accounts," he said meaningfully, his gaze going to Jo.

"Are you still harping on my ledger?" She grinned at him. There was a smudge of flour on her chin, and Chase felt an urge to get up, walk over, and wipe it off.

Mo gave a deep groan of frustration. He slowly shook his head and looked at Chase. "Have you ever had the pleasure of trying to decipher the bookkeeping methods of a woman?"

"Can't say I have," Chase admitted with a grin. "Is it that bad?"

"Worse. My esteemed client Ms. Benoit enters

bean sprouts and 'a trip' as expenses, without the slightest explanation of their importance to her profession, and then she expects me to wave a magic wand and come up with the answer."

Jo quickly came to her own defense, and the argument began. Chase sat back and watched the two combatants square off. Mo's meaningless insults were neatly countered by Jo's unique way of turning a straightforward question or statement into a jumbled response that a genius couldn't figure out. Chase was surprised to find himself jealous of the easy relationship they seemed to enjoy. It only brought home more clearly the sense of emptiness in his own life, an emptiness he was beginning to find distasteful. After a polite length of time, he excused himself and went home.

Later that evening, after Bink was in bed, Jake began his usual interrogation of Chase.

"How long do you plan on honoring us with your presence this time?" the burly ex-sergeant asked as he watched Chase pour his fourth scotch.

Chase regarded him levelly before raising the glass to his mouth and taking a sip of the drink. "I think I've finally lost my wanderlust, Jake."

"Well, it's about time. I was beginning to think you'd forgotten you had a son, much less a home. What does your family think?"

"They don't know."

"That should prove interesting," Jake muttered.

"Don't you think they'll be overjoyed to find

themselves saddled with me?" Chase gave a humorless laugh as he dropped back down into the overstuffed chair.

"Not if you plan on pickling your brain every night with scotch. What the hell's gotten into you, Chase? I've known you for fifteen years, and you've never drunk like this."

"Damned if I know, Jake," Chase said slowly, his gaze riveted to the amber liquid in the glass. "Damned if I know."

That wasn't the answer Jake was looking for, and his weathered brow wrinkled in puzzlement. It must be a woman, he thought, gazing into space. Chase always got prickly when he was involved with a woman. "Did you have much of a social life on this last job?"

Chase favored his friend with a wicked grin. "There is no woman, Jake, no special one, that is. I still like them all, so stop overtaxing your brain with worry that I'll unload one of my 'lady friends,' as you call them, on you."

"Well, now." Jake pulled at his chin. "If I were young and single, I do believe I'd look no farther than next door. Which apparently you did this afternoon. What do you think of Jo?"

"Don't start making plans to pair me off with the widow Benoit," Chase said determinedly.

"Widow!" Jake exclaimed. "Who on earth told you that?"

"She did." Chase chuckled. "Right after we finished discussing my posing nude for her!"

Jake was thunderstruck. His short, portly body was all but quivering with anger. "And to think I had her pegged as a sweet, innocent little thing."

"Which she is," Chase pacified him. "She's also dopey, naive, and a complete featherhead. Five minutes in her company and I thought my mind was going to explode."

"What about her husband?"

"Apparently he couldn't take her either. They were getting a divorce. Unfortunately, before the poor bugger had a chance to make a new life for himself, he choked to death on a piece of roast beef."

In the doctor's office, Jo finished dressing in record time, her palms wet with perspiration. She absolutely hated getting a physical examination, especially when it came to a pelvic. To her way of thinking, there was something ludicrous about a woman having to place one leg in a metal stirrup pointed toward the east and the other pointing toward the west, while the doctor bounced into the examining room and asked cheerfully, "How are you?"

Besides that, she silently grumbled as she reached underneath her skirt and pulled her blouse into place, her knees had a tendency to bang together like two tambourines. After giving herself a quick once-over in the small mirror behind the curtain, she left the examining room.

Dr. Marie Edderly was sitting at her desk when the nurse showed Jo in. She looked up and smiled. "Please sit down, Jo. I remember how much you dislike examinations."

"Well, at least it's over with for another year. Perhaps by then they will have come up with another form of torture." Jo sighed as she dropped into the leather chair. She clasped her hands in her lap and looked expectantly at her doctor, who was also a good friend. "So what's the verdict? Am I anemic again?"

"As a matter of fact, you are," Marie replied as she busied herself thumbing through Jo's file. "There are, however, one or two other little problems we need to discuss as well."

"Oh, boy." Jo grinned reluctantly. "Here comes the sermon on eating properly and getting adequate rest. Right?"

"Right."

"So give me my prescriptions and I'll be on my way. I have two stops to make before I get home, and it's already five o'clock."

Marie began scribbling on a pad, a peculiar expression on her attractive face. She sat back and regarded her patient. "There really isn't an easy way to tell you this."

"Tell me what?" Jo frowned. Lord! Was she

sicker than she'd imagined? Did she have some fatal disease?

"You're pregnant. From the size of your uterus I'd say approximately three months."

CHAPTER FOUR

By the time Jo left Dr. Edderly's office, she was convinced she was caught up in the middle of a bad dream. But dreams, she told herself as she left the building and began making her way to where her scooter was parked, usually were shrouded in a nebulous cloud of unreality. The fact that she was pregnant hadn't been cloudy or vague in the least, at least not to the doctor. Marie had been direct and to the point.

Babies were supposed to be a welcome addition to a family, she thought rather dazedly as she climbed aboard her scooter, their arrival into the world eagerly awaited by loving parents. But this baby she carried inside her now was the end result of an embittered man, who had looked upon the world as a giant playground created solely for his enjoyment. The thought of having children had been repugnant to Lance. It had been this aversion, along with several other habits and ideas revealed after they were married, that eventually caused Jo to decide her marriage was a failure.

It was a peculiar twist of fate, she thought wildly as she drove along. The pregnancy that her husband had refused for so long to give her had been granted, however unknowingly, in a moment of rage when revenge had been uppermost in his mind.

The events of the last time she'd seen Lance flashed through Jo's mind with the clarity of a movie on a wide screen. Their divorce was in its final stages when Lance called and asked her to go away with him to Las Vegas for the weekend. "I'm really down, Jo," he told her. "And even though we're almost divorced, does it have to mean we can't spend a weekend seeing some shows and just knocking around together?"

Jo had hesitated, honestly not knowing whether or not to accept the invitation. They certainly weren't mortal enemies, and even though she felt nothing for Lance but a kind of pity, who would it hurt? However, there was also the question of Vegas. Lance was a compulsive gambler. She broached the subject, only to have him brush it aside.

"I can handle it for two or three days." He gave a short, bitter laugh. "I suppose you think I'm some sort of nut for wanting to be with you, but for some strange reason I need that calmness that surrounds you. You've always had a knack for making me see myself for what I really am. Perhaps at this point in my life, that's exactly what I need."

"There will be separate rooms, of course," she'd stated, not wanting there to be the slightest misunderstanding between them. Giving him a few hours of her time was one thing, sharing his bed because he was at a low period in his life was another.

"Certainly," he replied unhesitatingly. "I suppose to anyone else our being together might be awkward. I don't believe you hate me, Jo, you just won't live with me anymore."

"No, Lance, I don't hate you." She wanted to add that she not only didn't hate him, she didn't feel anything for him, but that would have been unkind and she could tell from his voice that he was at an all-time low. She and Lance had been friends long before they married, and she assumed it was that relationship he was trying to recapture.

The wind was responsible for the added color in Jo's cheeks as she zoomed along on the scooter. Her mind wasn't really on her driving, evidenced by more than one blast of the horn from annoyed motorists when she sat unseeingly before traffic light after traffic light already turned green. Instinct guided Jo's hands as they manipulated the controls of the machine. Her mind was taken over with thoughts of the dismal failure of that weekend three months ago. Lance had tried to behave—or at least he had at first. But being a compulsive gambler and finding himself in one of his favorite haunts had proved more than he was capable of handling. On the first evening, as soon as they'd had dinner, he'd suggested that they just "peek" into the casino and watch a bit of the action. Jo didn't bother reminding him of his promise. That particular line had become standard stock during their marriage and she had no desire to recreate the scenario.

The "peek" turned into hours, with Lance losing heavily. Eventually Jo left him and returned to her room. There'd been no reproach on her part, nor any tearful pleadings for him to accompany her. The course of Lance's life had been set long before she met him. Acceptance of that, and the fact that whatever love she once felt for him was dead, had been the deciding factor in her filing for divorce.

The next morning a humble and contrite Lance appeared at her door, reminding Jo of a whipped puppy waiting for the traditional pat on the head and the perfunctory "Don't worry about it." Jo offered neither. There had to be caring and feeling in one person for another before concern could be present in their relationship. She felt nothing for Lance. Even pity had begun to fade. As the day wore on, he began to realize this wasn't the same Jo he thought he knew. She wasn't nearly as sympathetic to his moods and ideas as she'd once been. It was then that he finally accepted that not only was he soon to be out of Jo's life by means of the divorce, he was already out of her thoughts as a person. And that angered Lance.

During dinner that evening he was sullen and hostile. Afterward, he made no excuses when he left the table and headed for the casino. Jo returned to her room and began to pack for the trip home the next morning. Her packing finished, she dressed for bed and then watched television till her lids became heavy and sleep overtook her. The next thing she knew, Lance was bumping against the bedside table and falling across her thighs.

At first Jo was certain he was drunk. He had to be, she thought furiously as she struggled against his greater strength. But he hadn't been, and that fact alone was proof enough that Lance had deliberately forced himself on her.

As she came to a halt at a stop sign, Jo raised a trembling hand and brushed at the perspiration on her forehead. "Domestic rape" was the polite term society had chosen for what she'd experienced that night, she thought with grim cynicism totally out of character for her. But in Jo's mind there was nothing domestic about it. She had been raped as surely as if her assailant had been a perfect stranger. In essence he had been. Lance had become a stranger to her emotionally. She no longer loved him, no longer felt the gut-wrenching dread when he gambled away large sums of money, no longer felt compelled to make excuses to friends or family for his habit. It had been close to ten months since they'd separated, and even before that the physical side of their relationship had steadily deteriorated.

Six weeks later the news of Lance's death failed to evoke the tiniest bit of sorrow. Her only regret was that a man in his prime—another human being—had died uselessly.

She eased the scooter into the right lane for the last three blocks home, her mind attempting to grapple with this latest upheaval in her life. Lance hated children—and she was carrying his child in her womb. She'd felt nothing for him at the time of his death . . . now she was to be reminded of that painful humiliation a woman knows when she has been sexually abused.

By the time she finally arrived home, Jo imagined herself undergoing the same changes a volcano must experience before it erupts. It seemed as though she were barely holding herself in check, and at any moment she would explode. Being told she was pregnant had caused a multitude of old hurts to surface. Resentment, anger, and a number of other emotions she thought she'd learned to deal with all boiled near the surface. There was also the soon to be pressing problem of the baby. As much as she'd begged Lance to start a family during the early months of their marriage, she now wondered if she could love a baby conceived under such circumstances as this one had been.

A sudden bone-chilling thought occurred to her.

There was always abortion. Not so fast, a tiny voice of caution warned. You've completed the first trimester of your pregnancy. An abortion at this stage is out of the question.

Jo slumped back against the edge of the kitchen counter, her hands unconsciously moving to her stomach. So much for what she thought would be a quick and thorough solution to her problem. It would have been a difficult decision for her to make anyway.

A short gasp of frustration burst from her as she struggled to calm herself. She went through the motions of adding water to the tea kettle and setting it on the stove. Then she got out a tea bag and a bright yellow mug with a gay, red flower painted on one side. Suddenly her hands became still, and a thoughtful frown settled over her face. She needed something stronger than tea. With movements now more determined than controlled, Jo returned the mug and tea bag to their respective places, switched off the burner beneath the kettle, and proceeded to pour herself a glass of wine. The fact that she held her liquor—even an innocent glass of wine—about as effectively as a wet noodle failed to hinder her in the slightest. Neither did the well-publicized fact that pregnant women should refrain from alcoholic beverages.

Suddenly she wanted to revert to her childhood habit of simply changing identities when the unpleasantness of life threatened to overwhelm her.

And with that same wistful desire came the need to cry on a shoulder.

Tears filled the gray pools of her eyes as she contemplated the drink she was holding. "I'm not a coward," she whispered, the pink tip of her tongue touching her lips to taste the salty tears that eased unrestrained down her cheeks. "I just need time . . . a few hours to think. A few hours to accept the inevitable."

In those few moments as she attempted to reassure herself, the pleasant cream-and-blue kitchen took on the unmistakable aura of a prison. Jo could almost feel the four walls closing in on her. She turned and hurried out the door to the deck, drawing huge gulps of fresh air into her lungs. She made her way to the table and sat down, then let her head drop back against the chair. Get hold of yourself, a voice inside her head cautioned. You've always liked babies, you've always wanted at least six of your own. Why not start with this one?

The answer came racing front and center in her mind without the slightest effort on her part. The babies she wanted would be the result of two people's love for each other, a love that would surround and nurture them forever. This baby's creation was the result of an act of revenge committed against her body and her spirit. An act that was meant to be humiliating, that was meant to drag her down to the same depths of emotional misery Lance had felt.

Jo raised the glass to her lips and swallowed quickly. Her gaze fastened on the horizon and the blue and pale orange reflections of sunset. How lovely, she thought, her mind desperately reaching out for a release from the trauma surrounding her. She wanted to block out the immediate future and erase the past. For one incredible moment she was tempted to get her paints and brushes and capture the solitude, the beauty her eyes were seeing. Tomorrow, she promised herself, tomorrow I'll set up an easel on the deck and paint the sunset.

And will painting one sunset or ten thousand sunsets bring you any closer to a decision? her conscience prodded. Will it, with its glorious beauty, help you learn to love the baby you are carrying? Will that beauty help you to realize that there can be beauty and grace in every one of God's creations, regardless of their beginnings?

"Yoo-hoo. Anybody home?"

Jo remained perfectly still, her eyes tightly closed, hoping the intruder would go away. But the sound of brisk footsteps coming along the driveway toward the back of the house gave her reason to believe her hopes were in vain.

"So this is where you're hiding," Mary Clare Brent, partner and friend, remarked as she stepped onto the deck, then walked over and sat down opposite Jo. "I tried to call you several times this afternoon, but you weren't in. Were you out or were you just not answering your phone?" the tall, statuesque blonde asked, her sharp blue gaze taking in the almost empty wine glass and the paleness of Jo's features.

"I was out," Jo said quietly. She pushed herself up straighter in the chair. "Would you care for a drink?"

"As a matter of fact, I would. Keep your seat." She waved Jo back down in her chair. "I know where everything is. Can I fix something for you?"

"Please, another glass of wine. It's in the fridge." She knew from experience that the only way to get rid of Mary Clare was to sit and listen for a half hour or so. Jo knew, too, that sooner or later she would have to acquaint both her business associates with her problem. But for the moment she only wanted to be left alone.

The sound of banging cupboard doors in the kitchen failed to bring the slightest reaction from Jo. Nor did Chase's tall, tanned figure as he stepped out onto the patio next door, casually nodding toward his neighbor. When she failed to respond, he frowned. What the hell was wrong with her now? he thought irritably. She was looking straight at him. Suddenly Jo was joined by a tall blond beauty who brought a look of measured appreciation from Chase. He stared for a minute longer, then walked over to his car. He didn't have time to waste ogling his neighbor or her guest. His mother was waiting for him and he didn't want to be late. On the other hand, he thought with a grin as he drove away, he would remember to mention the blonde to Jo the next time he saw her. Though, of course, any reference to her sexy friend would come *after* he'd learned what Jo had found out from her visit to the doctor.

Sybil Colbern sat across the wrought-iron table from her oldest son, her eyes, the same startling blue as his, running lovingly over each inch of him. "So," she said softly, "are you really home for good, Chase?"

He tipped his head and grinned. " 'Fraid so, Mom. Think you can stand seeing my ugly puss more than two or three times a year?"

She reached across and tapped him smartly on the hand. "Don't you dare talk that way. Your father and I have dreamed of the day when you would stop roaming the world and settle down."

"Are you sure Dad's been dreaming of that day, Mom?" Chase chuckled.

"Well"—her soft laughter mingled with his— "he might have to get used to taking a tranquilizer now and then, but you can be assured he's glad to have you back. So is Bink." She shook her head fondly. "Oh, Chase, he's such a fine boy."

"And?" he prompted, waiting for that final "motherly" shoe to drop.

"And?" she asked innocently.

"Aren't you just dying to remind me that he is

62

without a mother and that it's my duty to provide him with one at the first available moment?"

Sybil looked straight at her son, her expression as stern as his. "Name one time when I've ever tried to meddle in your life or Bink's."

Chase gave her a sheepish grin, his gaze dropping to the half-finished scotch and water before him on the table. "Now that you mention it, I can't think of a single time. I'm sorry. It's just that everyone I've run into today has been quick to point out to me that I'm not getting any younger. They hurry to tell me that Bink is growing up without a woman's touch in his life. Hell, Mom, you'd think I was committing some sort of crime for not grabbing some gal and rushing her to the altar."

"Well, you're not," his mother said without the slightest fanfare. "Bink has been very adequately cared for by you and Jake. I really can't say whether or not he's missed having a mother. I know I've always tried to see that he was included in each family gathering we've had, and I've made a point of taking him on special outings when there was only the two of us." She gazed into space, a thoughtful expression on her face. "I honestly don't think Bink would appreciate your marrying only for his sake."

"You really do care for that grandson of yours, don't you?" Chase teased her.

That took the conversation into other areas, and

it was some time later when Chase mentioned Jo Benoit. "I understand from Bink that you like her."

"Oh, I do!" Sybil smiled. "She seems like such a gentle person. To be quite honest, Chase, for a while there Bink had a crush on that young woman. But I think that's worn off. Fortunately, she handled the situation very well, and now they seem to be good friends. But what about you? What do you think of her?"

"Er . . . I find her a bit flaky, but harmless enough. I would like to wean Bink away from her, though. After all, she's single, and her life-style is probably not geared to a kid Bink's age hanging around." What was the point in revealing that "calm Jo" was as screwy as a three-dollar bill? His mother was the most trusting soul in the world. Without his father to look after her, she would be the biggest soft touch for every derelict in the world. Funny, he thought as he watched his mother's face in the early shadows of dusk, there was something about her, heaven forbid, that reminded him of Jo Benoit.

Before that bizarre thought could go any further, Chase's father joined them. Talk turned to several different jobs the firm had going and to Chase's arrival in the office on Monday.

By the time he left his parents' home, Chase felt a little less tense about his decision to take a desk job. Although, to be honest, only time would tell if he'd done the right thing. But right or wrong, he knew he had to be around for Bink. The boy was fast approaching an age when he needed a father in person rather than one who put in an appearance only a few times during the year.

During dinner at home that night, Bink asked Jake if he thought Jo missed Satan.

"I'm sure she does," the older man admitted. "She raised him from a kitten."

"Who or what is Satan?" Chase asked, wondering what other little surprise was waiting for him next door.

"Jo's cat, Dad," Bink informed him. "He was huge and weighed at least fifteen pounds. He got into a terrible fight and had to have lots and lots of stitches. Jo hoped that would teach him a lesson and cut down on his tomcattin' at night, but it didn't. Satan liked to rumble. He staked out his territory, and he had to defend it. One night he didn't come home. Jo hasn't seen him since."

"How did you get to be such an expert on cats?" Chase grinned.

"From Jo. It's really simple. Ol' Satan was greedy; he wanted all the female cats in his territory for his harem."

Chase shot Jake a suspicious look, but the burly ex-sergeant ignored it and continued to calmly inhale the chicken and potatoes on his plate. "Jo seems to be pretty busy, Bink," Chase pointed out. "I don't want you getting in her way. Just because she does most of her work at home doesn't mean she has a lot of free time on her hands." Chase tried to establish a beginning for weaning his son away from their neighbor.

Unfortunately for his peace of mind, their neighbor had had more time with Bink than Chase had. It was clear his son would not be easily swayed, he decided grimly as he listened to Bink relate the schedule Jo worked by.

"And without anyone else in the house with her, Dad, there are times when she really needs a man around," Bink explained. "Course"—he smiled sheepishly—"since you've been home, I haven't been over at Jo's as much as usual. Once you get settled in, though, things will probably get back to how they used to be."

"Oh, I wouldn't worry too much about helping Jo," Chase said casually. "This is your summer vacation, son. It's a time for camp and fishing and all the other things you enjoyed before Jo moved next door. Besides, if the lady needs help, Jake or I will be here."

"I suppose you're right," Bink said thoughtfully. "But I wouldn't want to desert her completely, you know. Jo's special, Dad. She kinda reminds me of Grandma—sort of flaky, if you know what I mean?"

Jake gave a snort of amusement, and even Chase had to laugh at the comparison. "I do indeed know what you mean, Bink. That same thought occurred to me this afternoon when I was visiting with your grandmother. Thing is, though, when you're dealing with a . . . er . . . flaky individual, you have to be very careful. They think they make perfect sense. You can hurt their feelings if you let them know that what they do quite often doesn't make any sense at all. Do you know what I'm talking about?"

"Sure, Dad, I know. Like Grandma taking me to see all those Disney movies. Some of them are okay, but lots of them are for little kids. I didn't want to hurt her feelings, so I pretended to like them. And even Jo. She's got it in her head that I'm deprived because I don't have a mother, so she's always making cookies. To tell you the truth, I'm so sick of oatmeal cookies, I could croak. I always eat a bunch of them to make her happy, and she thinks I like them, so she keeps on making them. She even packs them up and sends them home with me. Now all my *friends* are tired of oatmeal cookies too!"

"Perhaps I can help you out there, Bink," Jake said with a chuckle. "I'll give her a different recipe. How about chocolate chip?"

"Great!"

"I'll take care of it tomorrow. Oh, and remember. Tomorrow is also the day you usually cut her grass. I know you've repaid your debt for the window, but I don't think it will hurt you to do a little mowing." He looked at Chase with a wicked gleam in his eyes. "Unless your dad plans on relieving you of that chore?"

"How about it, Dad?" Bink grinned. "Are you going to do what Jake said?"

"Jake is a busybody." Chase frowned at the older man. "But since mowing Ms. Benoit's grass seems to be the punishment for breaking her windows, I'll do it. It might be cheaper in the long run, however, to move the basketball goal."

Bink gave Jake a thumbs-up sign and tore from the room before his dad could change his mind. Chase eyed his companion, then got up from the table and walked into the kitchen that was separated from the breakfast area by a bar. "Exactly how long am I required to mow grass for breaking one lousy window?" he asked curtly as he poured a scotch and water.

"Three weeks," Jake told him. "And I think it's a fine thing you are doing, Chase. Mowing the grass, that is, not putting your damn brain to sleep with alcohol."

"You're beginning to sound like a record stuck in a groove, Jake." Chase walked back over and sat down at the table, his long legs stretched out before him. Their many years together and a deep friendship cushioned the stinging remarks they hurled at each other from time to time.

But in this particular instance, Jake was worried. He'd seen Chase through a number of ups and downs during the course of their friendship, but drinking had never been one of the problems. He rubbed a thick hand over his stubborn chin, his direct gaze never wavering. "How soon will you start work?"

"I'm supposed to go in Monday."

"Are you looking forward to it?"

"About as much as I would be if I were going to the dentist."

"Give it time, Chase," Jake suggested. "You might find that after a while you'll come to like it."

"I appreciate the concern, Jake." Chase gave him a wry grin. "And I know what you're trying to do. You're a good friend. But don't worry, I'm not an alcoholic—yet. Even though I detest being tied to a desk, I'll do it in order to be near Bink. Does that make you happy?"

"Of course." Jake gave all the appearances of being totally unconcerned, but underneath that scowling facade, he was grinning to himself. The initial step in his plan for Chase's future seemed to be coming along nicely. The next phase might prove a tad more complicated, he thought as he began to clear the table. It might indeed. He'd never considered himself in the role of cupid, but as far as he was concerned, Jo Benoit seemed to be the perfect match for Chase. She and Bink got along real well, and so would she and Chase if Jake could only figure out a way to bring them together.

He'd already heard Chase say that Jo was flaky, and he knew that might be a difficult obstacle to overcome at first. As far as looks went though, Jo was just as pretty as any of the other women he'd seen Chase with over the years. No, what was needed to pull Chase and Jo together was a crisis. Now, what sort of situation could he stir up that would help his "cause" along? he wondered.

CHAPTER FIVE

Jo poked at the chicken salad with her fork. The small bite she had in her mouth seemed to grow with each passing second. She simply didn't have an appetite. It had vanished earlier in the afternoon when she learned she was pregnant.

The visit with Mary Clare hadn't gone as she'd first thought. Though she'd hated doing it, she told Mary Clare about the weekend with Lance and that she was pregnant. Since they were so closely involved in each others' lives via the business, it seemed the decent thing to do. Surprisingly, her friend hadn't reacted with her usual opinionated attitude. Hearing Jo's story had shocked the attractive blonde. She'd never had to think of anyone but herself, let alone a baby. For once she was strangely silent.

For that, she was thankful, Jo thought as she dropped the fork and reached for the glass of iced tea. Advice from anyone at this particular moment in her life was the last thing she needed. A decision such as the one facing her wasn't something that could be decided by friends or family.

There was a frown worrying the delicate features of her face as Jo got up from the table and began clearing away the remains of her light supper. What she really needed was a long walk. Her shoulders and back were stiff with tension. But a quick look at the heavy darkness outside forced her to forget that idea. She thought instead of the new piece of exercise equipment she'd bought a few days earlier. That might help to ease the tension she was feeling. Mo had put it together for her the evening before, telling her in his abrupt manner that it reminded him of a damn torture rack.

A halfhearted smile tugged at her lips a short time later as Jo entered her studio. She walked over and stared at the contraption that was touted by its distributors as being "the perfect machine" to keep one's body fit and trim. Mo was right, it did indeed look rather strange, though she was convinced a good, brisk workout followed by a warm soak in the tub would do wonders for her.

After a brief glance at the instructions, which seemed so simple a first-grader could understand them, she sat down on the padded seat. She set the instruction sheet on the floor beside her. Careful to follow each step as written, she placed first one foot and then the other in the appointed places, then buckled a leather strap around each ankle. She pushed her legs forward and back in a rowing motion. So far so good. Next she lay back on the padded body support board and forced her hands beneath wide rubber strips and grasped hand grips on either side. According to the instructions, when she stretched out her legs, that movement would cause the arm mechanisms to extend over her head and back as well. Jo tested the procedure hesitantly at first, becoming more confident as she found the rhythm that suited her. She wasn't aiming for a record of endurance, simply a pattern of movement that would help alleviate the tension that had left her shoulders and back feeling as though a vise were squeezing her.

As the moments rushed by, Jo tried to clear her mind of all thought, recalling and applying the practice she'd learned during a course on mind control she'd taken several months ago. "Clear your mind," the instructor had lectured. "Let your body and mind become one. Imagine your thoughts and anxieties bursting free of the boundaries of your mind and let them go into the universe."

Jo closed her eyes and concentrated on centering herself. She imagined herself as an eagle, her arms becoming wings as she soared through the air, the mountaintops below her becoming nothing more than tiny hillocks. Up—up—she flew, exhilarating in the feel of the wind as it caressed her face, glorying in the oneness with nature that had permeated her entire being.

Suddenly the eagle's wings became rigid, its legs extended in preparation for landing. But Jo fought against this intrusion. She told herself she wasn't ready to give up this idyllic respite she'd become lost in. She shifted her powers of thought into overdrive, determined to remain a free spirit for a while longer. Unfortunately, no amount of imagining herself soaring through the air seemed to work.

With a painful rush of reality sweeping over her, Jo was forced to view the situation in the same calm manner that had always ruled her life. She opened her eyes, raised her head, and surveyed the position of her legs and arms. She almost grinned in spite of her predicament. She looked like the lone survivor of an Indian attack, staked out and left on the desert to die.

Heaving a huge sigh of resignation, she placed her thumb against the end of the hand grip, as per the instructions, and pressed. That action would trigger a lever and would, in turn, loosen the bands around her wrists. When the bands failed to loosen, however, Jo frowned and pressed harder. Nothing happened. She looked down at her feet, seeking an alternate escape route, but her ankles were snugly strapped into place.

She dropped her head back against the padded support, her fruitful imagination conjuring up all sorts of headlines in the paper and on television regarding her rather peculiar demise on an exercise machine. "Promising Young Artist Found Dead In Bizarre Circumstances." "Young Widow Believed To Have Been The Victim Of An Insanely Jealous

Lover." "Could Drug-Induced Sex Orgy Be The Motive Behind Pregnant Artist's Death?"

One thing was sure, Jo decided as she struggled to free herself, her parents would be too embarrassed even to attend her funeral. Her mother would be ready to believe the very worst about her youngest child, and while the rest of the family might have different opinions about the shameful cause of death, they would side with her mother.

Exasperation, mingled with the beginnings of panic, edged its way into Jo's mind. "Damn!" she exclaimed, her humor evaporating as she was forced to accept how very precarious a situation she was caught in.

Why doesn't someone come? she wondered, remembering the number of times she'd been interrupted in her work by unexpected visits from friends. Why the devil couldn't one of them decide to drop by this evening? But no matter how much she longed to hear the sound of the doorbell, the house was silent as a tomb.

There were tears of frustration in her smoky gray eyes some time later when Jo thought she heard a distinct knock on the back door off the deck. She raised her head in an effort to hear better, wondering if her mind was playing tricks on her. But no, there it was again. Not only was someone knocking, they were jiggling the doorknob as well.

Never being one to let opportunity slip through

her fingers, Jo yelled at the top of her lungs, "Help!"

"Jo?" came a deep, questioning voice. "Where the hell are you?"

"In my studio," she screamed. She lapsed into silence as she heard heavy footsteps move across the deck and then several well-chosen oaths as her rescuer became acquainted with the rosebushes planted beneath the window of the studio.

When Chase Colbern's face appeared on the other side of the glass, his expression swiftly changed from caution to disbelief. He stared at the strange position of his neighbor, then wondered what the hell she was up to. He'd distinctly heard her call for help, but from the looks of things, it wasn't help she needed. A slow angry fire began to surge through him as he saw how her breasts were straining against the skimpy halter and how the satiny smoothness of her legs was set off to perfection by the red shorts she was wearing.

Didn't the damn woman ever give up? First she'd attacked him with a motor scooter, then she'd invited him to pose nude for her, and now she was calmly reclining in a pose guaranteed to make any man's temperature shoot through the roof. Judging from the layout, he thought furiously, she probably had the whips and other little articles of her trade tucked away in the closet.

"Obviously you were expecting someone else,

Ms. Benoit," he roared at her through the closed window.

"I was?" Jo cried out uncomprehendingly. What on earth was wrong with the man? she thought dizzily. Couldn't he see that she was trussed up like a turkey? Her heart thumped crazily when she saw him start to turn away. "Wait!" she yelled. "I need help."

"You sure as hell do, lady," Chase retorted, glaring at her, "but not from me. I'll admit I've never cared much for shrinking violets, but even for me, you're too much."

"Chase! Mr. Colbern!" Jo said quickly, something in her voice stopping him. "I honestly don't know what you're talking about and I'll be happy to discuss it with you later, but at the moment, I need your help. I can't get off this thing."

"You *what?*" came the bellowing response, incredulity slowly settling over his features.

"I'm stuck—or rather this blasted machine is stuck." She shook her head in frustration. "Please, try to get in here and help me. I'm tired of shouting at you through the window."

"Do you keep this locked?" He tapped one long forefinger against a pane of glass. No longer was there scorn or disgust in Chase's voice. He wasn't sure just how she'd managed it, but the damn, daffy woman really *was* stuck on that exercise machine.

"Yes, but I think the one in the breakfast area is

unlocked." She gave him a weak smile. "Would you mind hurrying?"

The entire time Chase was attempting to squeeze the width and breadth of his large body through a window built more on Bink's scale, he was cursing a blue streak, his thoughts toward his irritating neighbor less than charitable. Christ! All he'd wanted to do was come home and be with his son. He didn't want this annoying woman next door. She was trouble. He had known she would be from the first moment he'd seen that heart-shaped face and those soft pink lips. And her eyes, he thought defeatedly. A man could drown in those gray pools.

Drowning in gray pools of ecstasy was about the last thing on his mind, however, as Chase entered the studio moments later. He came to a halt just inside the room, struggling to control his laughter as he stared at the sight before him. "Er—were you attempting to set a new endurance record?" he asked in a wobbly voice, barely able to contain his mirth.

"Nothing so noble, I assure you," Jo said quietly. "This is supposed to be the very latest in exercise equipment. Using it is suppose to take the place of jogging or long walks."

Chase walked over, then went down on his knees beside her, his fingers working at the wide rubber strip holding her wrist in place. "Well, it looks to me, Ms. Benoit, as though you'd do better sticking with the real thing."

"Perhaps I should have bought just the rowing machine," Jo said thoughtfully. "But this seemed ideal for the stiffness I get in my shoulders from sitting so long over my drafting table."

"I'm sure Mo or one of your other men friends would be glad to massage that tension away," Chase said sarcastically. He moved down and released her feet, then did the same for the other hand.

Jo sat up, her fingers busily rubbing her wrists. "Are you implying that I have men dropping in round the clock?" Really, Chase Colbern seemed blessed with an imagination almost as fruitful as her own.

"I'm not implying anything, Ms. Benoit." He frowned as he rose to his very formidable height, his cool gaze sweeping her from head to toe. "But, you must admit, you do lead a very . . . colorful . . . life."

"Oh? What makes you say that?" Jo got to her feet, feeling rather lightheaded from having lain in a prone position for so long.

"Are you all right?" Chase asked, seeing how unsteady she was. He reached out and caught her by the elbow and led her to the only chair in the room. "Did you go to the doctor like you promised me?" Now why the hell had he asked that? The last thing he wanted was to become involved in this woman's life. Why did she have to look so damn innocent, and why did he feel some inexplicable urge to protect her? It made no sense, no sense at all.

A short, mirthless chuckle escaped Jo as she leaned back in the chair and stared at this giant standing before her. "Oh, I definitely kept my promise, Chase."

"And?" he prodded.

"Are you planning on living next door for an indefinite period or are you thinking of moving?" she asked.

"What the hell's that got to do with you going to the doctor?"

"Well?" Jo demanded. "Are you?"

"Of course I'm not moving," he said disgustedly. "This is a nice, quiet neighborhood. It's a good place to raise my son."

Jo shrugged. "That's too bad." For some reason she'd hoped she wouldn't have to tell Chase that she was pregnant. From some of the remarks he'd made, she had a fairly good idea he wasn't too fond of her. Coming up pregnant would only make matters worse between them. "I'm pregnant."

"You're what?" he exploded in a shocked voice.

"Pregnant. In the family way, as my grandmother used to say. Whatever you wish to call it."

"How?"

"How what?" she looked at him crazily. Heavens! For a grown man, he was incredibly dense.

80

"How did you get pregnant?"

"The usual way, I assure you," Jo said quietly. "Or rather, the biological manner in which a sperm and an egg met was usual. The rest wasn't usual. I was raped." She saw Chase turn pale, saw him reach out and grasp the edge of the drafting table to steady himself. Immediately Jo got to her feet. "Would you like to sit down? You don't look well." Maybe she should have been less blunt in telling him. Maybe she shouldn't have told him at all, she thought miserably. But there were Bink and Jake to consider and, in the long run, Chase himself. She wasn't blind to the subtle jabs he aimed her way from time to time, and there was something about their coming from Chase that bothered her. She didn't want this man to think of her as the sort of woman who slept with every man that came along.

Chase stared at her as if she'd lost her mind. God! he thought wildly. Not only had she calmly told him she was pregnant, but that she had been raped. Suddenly he wanted the security of some dangerous assignment with bullets zinging past his ears, with running footsteps chasing him. Anything would be more welcome than what he envisioned the next few months to be. And Bink! How on earth was he going to explain this to his son?

"I need a drink," he croaked hoarsely.

"Of course," Jo replied soberly. "Come with me," she offered, leading the way to the kitchen.

81

In the kitchen, Chase slumped into a chair, his dazed eyes following Jo as she got out glasses and ice. When she turned and looked questioningly at him, he said faintly, "Scotch on the rocks." The drink materialized before him only seconds later, but Chase didn't immediately taste it. Instead he looked hard at the glass of wine Jo had fixed for herself. Without thinking, he leaned over and removed the drink from her hand. "It's been a long time since I was around a pregnant woman, but even I know that you aren't supposed to drink alcohol."

"An occasional glass of wine isn't likely to hurt," she said stubbornly, reaching for the glass. A light slap against her hand was all she got for her effort. "I appreciate your concern, Mr. Colbern, but I do think I'm capable of looking after myself."

"Really?" Chase muttered dryly after downing nearly his entire drink. "I'd say the subject is debatable." He sat forward, his thick forearms resting on the edge of the table, his broad shoulders hunched. "What were the police able to do?"

"About what?" Jo looked puzzled.

Chase closed his eyes briefly and shook his head as if to clear his brain. Talking to this woman was like trying to find one's way out of a maze on a pitch-black night in a pea soup fog. "What did the police do when you reported the rape?" he said slowly, carefully enunciating each word.

Jo leaned toward him. "I did not report the rape to the police," she replied in the same pointed manner he'd used in posing the question.

"Why the hell not?" he all but yelled.

"Because there is very little that can be done when the rapist is one's husband. I don't believe there is more than one—possibly two—states that have laws protecting a wife under such circumstances."

"You mean it was—Lance? It was Lance? Your husband?"

"Yes."

"Did he force his way into the house?"

"No, not the house. He forced his way into my room at the hotel where we were spending the weekend."

"Now wait a minute." Chase turned his head and gave her a slanted look. "If you were spending the weekend together, how the hell can you call it rape?"

"Perhaps if you put the brakes on that speeding brain of yours and listen for a change, I just might be able to explain what happened."

"Go ahead." Chase scowled. "Why shouldn't I listen?" He spoke as if he were alone. "Not one single thing about you has made any sense from the moment I met you." He waved one large hand in a magnanimous gesture. "Talk, speak. I'm certain I'll be just as confused when you're finished as I am now."

"Well, you won't be, Chase, if you keep an open mind," Jo pointed out. She told him the whole story then, watching his face for the tiniest glimmer of understanding. But looking for comfort in his rock-hard features, she decided, was comparable to gaining a smile from the faces on Mount Rushmore. When she finished, she sat nervously, waiting for him to speak.

Finally, after what seemed like an eternity, Chase lifted one shoulder in an apologetic shrug. "I'm sorry," he began gruffly. "It was a rotten thing to have happen to you."

"Do you really believe me?" Jo asked curiously.

Chase stared at her, his gaze steady and direct. "I believe you."

"Thank you." She inhaled shakily. "Frankly, when the doctor told me this afternoon that I was pregnant, I almost didn't believe it myself . . . I mean the way it happened. I've worked very hard putting that night out of my mind, and I simply wasn't prepared to relive it again. Does that make any sense?"

"Yes, it does," Chase said softly. He reached out and caught her hand in his. "Have you thought of getting help? I mean, there are all sorts of organizations now that deal with problems such as yours."

"I've thought about it." Her tone was dry and brittle, and Chase could see the pain in her eyes. "But from what I've read and heard, my particular case isn't as important—or perhaps I should say devastating—as many others. I wasn't assaulted by a stranger, was I? I also went away with him of my own free will. So"—she sighed—"when all the circumstances are considered, you could say I brought it on myself."

"I've never heard a more ridiculous statement in my entire life," Chase said angrily. "First of all, it isn't uncommon for an estranged couple to see each other before the divorce is final. It happens all the time. People react to divorce in different ways. During that final period when they know that on a certain day that a part of their life will be changed, some panic. They find themselves wanting to reach out for that old security, for that one familiar person who will no longer be a part of their life. If a census were taken, you might be surprised at how many couples do the same thing you and Lance did. It isn't something to be ashamed of, honey. The problem in your case was Lance's inability to handle rejection."

"You make it all sound so simple." Jo smiled.

"That's because I can stand back and look objectively at the problem. You're directly involved. It's always easier for an outsider. But I think you need to try and put the past behind you, Jo. The important thing now is the baby. You do want to keep it, don't you?" Chase asked, the shrewd glint in his eyes like an accusing finger.

An electric silence hovered over the room as Jo

sought an answer. Talking with Chase was good. For all his gruffness and the sharpness of his tongue, she'd found a gentle streak in him. Could she possibly make him understand that keeping this baby would always remind her of the humiliation she'd suffered, not to mention having been a fool for trusting Lance?

Jo lowered her eyes without an answer for Chase.

CHAPTER SIX

Normally Chase liked the outdoors. That special enchantment drawn from fresh air and wide-open spaces had claimed him at an early age. But today he wasn't finding the same pleasure from the sun that he usually did. There simply wasn't an ounce of excitement in pushing a lawn mower back and forth across a yard, he thought disgustedly, his mouth down turned with displeasure. There was also another reason for the heavy scowl marking his face. Jo.

To his knowledge he'd never known a woman who had been raped. He found that the very idea of Lance Benoit, even though he was Jo's estranged husband, forcing himself on her in such a degrading manner left him wanting to strike out at someone. He wanted to smash his fist into the man's face. He wanted to inflict pain. Forcefully taking a woman was against everything Chase believed in, though he'd never really thought too much about it until two nights ago when he'd heard Jo's story.

And now, Chase fumed, the payment for that one moment of revenge gained by Lance had left Jo pregnant. Pregnant with a baby she wasn't sure she wanted. He pushed the lawn mower savagely. He'd known of some unfair tricks being played on people, but this one was about the worst.

Chase wondered how Bink would take the news. More important, how was he going to explain to his son that the woman he adored was expecting a child? And if she chose not to keep the baby, how would Bink feel about that?

God! he thought, groaning, he was beginning to worry about the darned woman as if she were his responsibility. Right, his conscience jabbed at him. You're acting like you're concerned for her. Don't you think you're overdoing it just a bit? Be reasonable, the voice continued. This is something she'll have to deal with herself. If she doesn't want the baby, then there are people out there who would give their right arm for a baby. Did you come back to Houston to play nursemaid to a pregnant widow?

Chase glared, almost jerking the handle off the machine he was wielding so mercilessly. A sudden movement caught his eye and he glanced up. Jake was standing on the patio, waving with one hand, the other hand holding two cold beers. Chase gave him a thumbs-up sign, turned off the mower, then walked over and joined him.

"I was never aware that mowing was one of

your favorite things to do," Jake said innocently as both men settled back in comfortable lounge chairs and took a long sip of cold beer.

"Jealous?" Chase countered. "Would you like to swap jobs? I don't mind trying my hand at running the house for a few days."

"Ha!" Jake snorted. "And a fine mess we'd be in if I were to take you up on that offer. The last time you 'took over' it took me damn nigh a month to find all the little ferret holes where you'd hidden things."

Chase grinned. "Just trying to be neighborly."

"Speaking of neighbors," Jake said thoughtfully. "Have you seen anything of Jo lately?"

"Er—not since night before last."

"Oh? I don't recall her coming over. Was it after I was in bed?"

"Yeah," Chase drawled, "it was. We waited until you were raising the rafters with your snoring, then we snuck into the house for our illicit meeting."

Jake ignored the needling. "It's not like Jo not to drop in at least once during the day. I wonder if she's sick."

"If you're that worried, why don't you walk over and check on her?" Chase suggested. Frankly, he was concerned himself. There hadn't been any movement around the house next door in a couple of days.

"I was about to suggest that same thing to you,"

Jake told him. "Jo's nice, and it wouldn't hurt you to get to know her better. Besides, she doesn't get out nearly enough for a young woman her age. I don't think I've seen her go out with a man more than two or three times since she's been living there. That's not normal."

"Perhaps she's patterning her life after you," Chase teased. Jake's bachelorhood had always been a great source of amusement to Chase. He knew for a fact that the older man was positively terrified of marriage. He would take a woman out to dinner from time to time, but nothing more. He considered Chase and Bink his family and devoted all his efforts to their welfare—whether they wanted it or not, Chase thought, chuckling inwardly.

"Stop trying to evade the issue," Jake snapped. "That poor girl could be lying over there sick—or worse. Where is your sense of duty?"

"Minding its business, exactly what yours should be doing," Chase remarked just as a red motor scooter whizzed into the driveway next door and into the garage. "What the hell?" he muttered, coming to the edge of his chair.

"What do you mean?" Jake gave him a curious look. "It's only Jo. At least we know she isn't ill, no thanks to you."

"Why don't you find a hobby, Jake? You've become paranoid in your old age." He set the empty beer can on the table, then got to his feet. "I think I'll finish mowing."

But it wasn't the mower or the lawn that drew Chase's immediate attention. His long stride made short shrift of the distance from his yard to Jo's back door, his expression thunderous. He raised his fist to pound on the door at the exact same moment it opened.

"Oh, my!" a startled Jo exclaimed as she quickly stepped back from his raised hand. "Is something wrong?"

"You're damn right it is," Chase yelled as he stepped inside and slammed the door shut behind him. He kept stalking a retreating Jo till she felt the edge of the kitchen counter pressing into her back. "Have you forgotten, madam, that you are pregnant?"

"Er—no—no, I haven't," she quickly assured him, her eyes wide with bewilderment.

"Have you forgotten that you have been having dizzy spells for the past few weeks?" he rapped out again.

Jo shook her head. "No, I haven't forgotten."

"Then will you please explain why I just saw you fly down your driveway on that damn motor scooter?"

"Why—why, I went to the supermarket," she stammered helplessly as she pointed to the bag of groceries behind her. "There's still more in the basket on the scooter."

"I'll get it," Chase answered tersely, then turned and stormed out the door.

Jo barely had time to remove a carton of skimmed milk from the bag when he barreled his way back in and thumped the remaining groceries onto the counter.

"What's that?" he eyed the milk as if it were contaminated.

"Milk," she said, glaring at him. Suddenly she was irked. Enough was enough. He needn't take his bad mood out on her. "It comes from a cow."

Chase brushed her words aside impatiently. "What are you doing with skimmed milk? That's not what you should be drinking!"

Jo grabbed the carton and practically threw it into the fridge. Turning, she favored her guest with a stormy glint in her eyes. "Would you mind leaving, Mr. Colbern? It's hot, I'm tired, and I really don't feel like fighting with you."

Chase held her gaze for several seconds, the rise and fall of his bare chest slowing as he brought his temper under control. Finally he gestured with one hand, the other going to the back of his neck. "Okay," he rasped, "I was out of line. I'm sorry. But don't you realize the danger you put yourself in when you ride that damn scooter in your condition?"

So that was it, Jo thought, amazed. He was concerned for her. That realization left her feeling strangely vulnerable. It occurred to her that she'd never had a man show concern for her, and, frankly, she'd never really wanted that sort of attention. Her only close relationship with a man had been with Lance, who had had enough problems to keep both their minds occupied.

"I've been riding the scooter for over a year now, and I really feel comfortable on it," she said quietly. "As long as I'm careful, I don't see any need to change." She waved Chase to a chair at the table, then sat down herself. "I'm sorry I snapped at you, but you took me by surprise, appearing at my door like that."

Chase hunched forward in the chair, his hands clasped in front of him on the table. He stared at the creamy smoothness of her skin, at the enchanting way her lashes grew straight, then turned up at the ends. Thick dark lashes, lending their own touch of excitement to eyes he found so mysterious. "It's not exactly your driving that worries me." He grinned, his smile crooked. "Although I do remember being rammed in the rear end by that damn scooter—"

"That was an accident," Jo was quick to defend herself.

"I'm sure it was, but there are other drivers on the road you have to contend with. And as anyone knows, good defensive driving is essential if a person is to survive. Besides that, if you were to skid or be hit by a car, there would be nothing to protect you. On that scooter, you're an accident just waiting to happen."

"You have several good arguments on your side," Jo conceded after a thoughtful pause. "However, at this point in time, I'm afraid I'm not ready to give up the scooter. Though I will start looking around for some alternate means of transportation," she hastened to add, seeing the angry set of Chase's jaw.

"A car," he stated stubbornly.

"Certainly a car."

"Then why didn't you say that to start with?"

"I said I would start looking—"

"For an alternate means of transportation," Chase scowled. "Knowing you, that could mean anything from a damn jackass to a tricycle."

On an impulse, Jo leaned over and patted his hands. "You look tired. Have you had lunch?" she asked with concern.

"I've been mowing. I was planning on grabbing a sandwich later."

"Then have one with me. Suddenly I'm ravenous." She smiled as she got to her feet, then walked over and began unpacking the brown bags.

Chase got up to help, finding it rather nice to be moving about the kitchen with a woman. Of course, he was quick to tell himself, it wasn't like engineering a dam, but he supposed such a relationship had its place in the scheme of things. Besides, he mused, there was something about Jo Benoit that caused things to fall into perspective. He didn't feel rushed or cornered when he was with her.

Without thinking, he began putting together his sandwich from the makings she'd set out on the counter, leaving her to concoct her own. He even nodded pleasantly to himself when he saw the cubed cheese she raked from the cutting board into the bowl with the apple slices and chopped celery. He would have preferred she eat more meat, but then, it was lunchtime. He was certain she would have meat at dinner. He made a mental note to check and make sure. If not, then he would bring her some of Jake's pot roast.

Chase was spreading mayo on the top slice of bread for his huge sandwich when an odor he had hated since childhood hit him. He glanced at the mixture Jo was stirring in a small bowl and almost gagged. "What the hell is that?" he roared.

"Cottage cheese and sauerkraut." Jo grinned at him. "Want a bite?"

"No! Are you honestly planning on eating that rotten stuff?" he asked disbelievingly.

"It is kind of weird, isn't it?" She shrugged as she continued stirring. "And to answer your question—yes, I am going to eat it. I've had the most awful craving for this . . . creation for days now. Can you believe it, I don't even get heartburn afterward."

"Why don't we eat out on the deck," Chase suggested. "That way I can sit down wind from you."

"That's very rude, you know."

"Your choice of food is very smelly."

"Well"—she looked at him, struggling to control her amusement—"I suppose since you are a guest, I'll have to abide by your wishes." She reached for a tray and added the food, napkins, and a fork for her own use. "Do you mind bringing the drinks? I think I'll have a glass of wine."

"I'll take care of it." Chase smiled grimly. But minutes later when he placed two large glasses of milk on the table on the deck, Jo frowned.

"I've already had my milk for the day," she said pleasantly. "I prefer wine with lunch."

Chase dropped into the chair opposite her, then regarded her with a no-nonsense look. "Unless you want your baby to be born severely underweight and zonked out on alcohol, you'll curtail your desire for wine, Ms. Benoit," he said crisply.

His words startled Jo. She was aware that an occasional glass of wine was acceptable. But she was also aware that prolonged use of any alcoholic beverage wasn't good for the baby. Suddenly it hit her. She couldn't think of only herself, she must consider the baby's welfare.

But I don't want to have to consider that, she argued with herself. I didn't ask for this baby, and I'm not sure I even want it. Ah-ha, her conscience zinged right back. Yesterday you were thinking you *didn't* want the baby. Today you are thinking you *might* not want it. Are you getting soft? Are you beginning to accept that having a baby might not be such a bad thing after all?

Without thinking, she reached for the glass of milk, raised it to her lips, and drank from it.

Chase didn't bother trying to make conversation. He knew from the look in her eyes that Jo was fighting a battle not only in her mind, but within her heart as well.

"You're very quiet." She finally spoke after several minutes had gone by.

"You seemed preoccupied." Chase watched her carefully as he spoke. "Do you have a family? I don't seem to remember Bink mentioning anyone."

"I have quite a large family actually. My parents, two brothers, and a sister."

"Have you told them about the baby?"

"Certainly not."

"Don't you think that's a little cruel? I mean, your parents have a right to know that they are going to have a grandchild. And I'm sure your sister would want to share this time with you. After all, you told me, and I'm a relative stranger."

"Not really, you know," Jo confessed, a rosy glow settling in her cheeks. "From the day I met Bink, I've heard so much about you. Probably a lot more than you think. But I suppose one of the main reasons I confided in you was Bink. He's almost thirteen, and even with all the liberal think-ing nowadays, I don't want him to think badly of me."

"I appreciate that." Chase nodded. "But I still think you're selling your family short."

"That only goes to show how little you know about them, Chase," Jo said slowly. "For starters, my mother will probably be furious that I was un-able to have an abortion. My father will more than likely look at me as if I've suddenly lost my mind, and my brothers and sister will share that opinion. They will then hold one of their councils of war and come to a decision as to what *they* think I should do."

"That doesn't sound like much of a family," Chase stated bluntly.

"Oh—they're not so bad. They just all seem to live in a different world from me. They're all bril-liant and have probably wondered on more than one occasion how I ever happened to be born into the family. I suspect—no," she corrected herself, "let me be perfectly honest. I *know* I've been a horrible disappointment to them. For me to come up pregnant, not to mention how I got pregnant, will be a severe blow to them."

"Then maybe you shouldn't tell them after all," Chase said gruffly. Hell, she needed all the support she could get at this point, not a damn bunch of stiff-necked idiots belittling her.

"Don't worry, Chase." She sounded confident.

"I've been handling my family for years. I'll tell them, they'll go into one of their huddles and decide what I'm to do, and I'll tell them to take a hike."

"That simple, huh?" He grinned, his admiration for her growing by the second. She might be a flake, and no bigger than his fist, but she had guts.

"A piece of cake." She smiled in return and popped a forkful of kraut and cottage cheese into her mouth.

CHAPTER SEVEN

As Jo closed and locked her back door, she fervently hoped Chase wasn't peering out the window at her. She was going to ride the motor scooter to her parents' home, and she hoped to do so without getting involved in an argument with her neighbor.

She'd half promised to start looking at cars after his explosive entrance into her kitchen several days before—and she would. Thing was, she thought stubbornly as she fastened the strap of the helmet and got on the scooter, she found herself resenting the changes her pregnancy had brought about in her life. But she couldn't decide if it was the baby or the fact that, in the final analysis, Lance had gotten back at her in a way that she was helpless to parry.

Jo knew, as she left the quiet street where she lived, that deep in her heart she was beginning to think of the baby as a real little person now. Wondering if it was a boy or a girl. Already it had changed from a faceless entity she'd at first refused to acknowledge, to a small bundle smelling of baby powder that she would hold in her arms.

There had been moments in the last few days when she'd found herself standing before shop windows where complete layettes were displayed. Somehow, the thought of giving the baby up for adoption seemed to be slipping farther and farther from her mind.

The care and tending of a baby would demand a large amount of her time, she told herself as she rode along, the wind turning her cheeks rosy. Time that she really didn't have. Why, there were days now when she wondered how she would ever meet the deadlines for some of her illustrations, much less complete the artwork for the greeting cards. No, she decided with a tiny shake of her head, a baby would play havoc with her life and her time. But even as she was congratulating herself on her sensible decision, another part of her was wondering exactly when she'd become such a coward.

Jo's arrival at her parents' home was met with the same degree of head shaking and tongue clucking as usual, which left her a little out of sorts. There was nothing whatsoever wrong with a motor scooter, she automatically defended her choice of transportation to her mother, even as the older woman was offering her cheek for the ceremonial kiss.

"But it looks so—so casual," Sarah Kincaid sighed. She was a small woman, only a half inch or so taller than her youngest daughter. Her face was relatively unlined, due to the dedicated care she lavished on her skin as well as her entire body. Her clothes, more often than not, bore designer labels and her hair was never mussed. Sarah had presented a perfect picture of elegance for as long as Jo could remember.

"I am casual, Mom." Jo smiled, unruffled by the criticism. "The scooter is also very economical to operate."

"Well, if it's money that you're worried about, I'd be more than happy to help you."

The scene that greeted Jo as she followed her mother into the den seemed not to have varied at all from her last visit. In fact, she told herself as she stood back for a moment and listened to the voices of her father, two brothers, and sister, it could quite possibly even be the same argument. It always struck Jo that the members of her clan attended Sarah's weekly dinners for the sole purpose of arguing.

Jo took a seat next to her sister, Elise, on the sofa, leaned back, and prepared herself for a boring evening. At least it would be boring till she dropped her little bomb about being pregnant.

Dinner was delicious, as it always was. Sarah wouldn't tolerate anything less. But the overstuffed feeling Jo had as a result of the rich food left her sleepy. She refused dessert, asking for an apple instead.

"Aren't you feeling well, dear?" her mother asked from her seat at the foot of the table. "You can have ice cream instead of custard if you'd prefer."

"An apple will be fine, Mom," Jo answered without fanfare as all eyes turned to her.

"Are you on a diet?" Elise asked. She considered dieting a health hazard. Exercise was her answer to a healthy body. Jo was convinced that one day they would find Elise had jogged herself to death.

"Not really, but I'm pretty sure I'll have to think about one fairly soon."

"I don't think diets are healthy," Elise stated.

"I disagree." Cal, her middle brother, spoke up. "But to be genuinely effective, you have to keep very strict records of daily weight and food intake. I have some good material on the subject, Jo. I'll get it to you."

"Thanks, Cal, but—"

"What you need to do, Jo," Edward, the eldest of the Kincaid offspring interrupted, "is join the health club I belong to. There's none of that damn jogging Elise is always doing or Cal's irritating charts and food intake to worry with."

"Do you have many pregnant women at your club, Edward?" Jo asked as she inspected the apple for the next best place to sink her teeth into. It was happening again. All evening she had tried to look for an easy way to tell them that she was pregnant, but she never had the chance. They were too busy being the all mighty authorities on every subject in

103

the world, brushing aside every comment she made as being silly or worse. Well, Jo reasoned, if the lot of them were so well organized, so well adjusted, how would they handle the news that an addition to the family was on the way?

Edward gave her a disgusted look. "It's hardly the place for an expectant mother."

"Good. That eliminates me then."

"What on earth is that remark supposed to mean?" Frank Kincaid asked, scowling.

"It means that in about six months, Dad, you are going to be a grandfather. Does the idea appeal to you?"

Her father sat stunned. Sarah turned a peculiar shade of gray, her hands gripping the arms of the chair. Elise was quiet, a delighted sparkle in her eyes. Edward sat as stiff as a wax dummy in a museum, and Cal immediately began muttering statistics about women Jo's age and the number of healthy babies they had.

For once it was Elise who showed a human side. "I suppose you'll have to start thinking of things like diapers and such, won't you?"

"True." Jo nodded, wondering what was coming next. This reaction was not at all what she'd expected from her sister.

"Would it be all right if I—er—if I maybe did a little shopping for you?"

"What a nice thought, Elise. I'd like that."

Jo didn't stay at the dinner table very long after

her announcement. She quietly explained that Lance was the baby's father, then said good-bye and slipped out the front door.

The trip back to her house was *made* quick. But as Jo zipped along, her thoughts were on the not-so-surprising way her family had acted. After they'd recovered from the initial shock, each one, except for Elise, had offered his opinion on what she should do. But even then, Jo realized, even with the raised voices of her family going on about her, she'd felt protective toward the baby growing inside her.

Strange, she mused as she neared her street. On the way to visit her folks, she'd congratulated herself on her decision that she didn't have time to bother with a baby. But as Jo had sat listening to the various arguments of her family, she'd found herself unconsciously defending the tiny life placed in her care. She'd even made a silent promise to herself never to interfere in her child's life.

Suddenly it hit her. *Her child!*

Not some common, everyday event occurring every second of every minute somewhere in the world. Not some faceless entity without feeling. This was *her* baby growing inside her. *Her baby.*

At first the phrase had a stiff, peculiar ring to it. But as Jo kept repeating it, it became easier and wasn't in the least distasteful. In fact, a feeling of warmth, mixed with a sense of possession, slowly stole over her.

"How much time can a tiny baby take, for Pete sake?" she muttered under her breath as she parked the scooter in the garage and released the strap of the helmet. She put one foot on the concrete floor of the garage and was about to turn, when the shadowy figure of a large man suddenly appeared in the double-doored opening. Jo opened her mouth to scream just as Chase's angry voice roared in her ears.

"So you finally decided to come home, did you?" he demanded. "Do you know what time it is?"

Jo glared at him, her fear quickly dissipating. Now she felt only anger. How dare he confront her like this, as if he were her keeper? "Well," she drawled irritably, "after the third or fourth singles' bar, I got bored, so I finally came home. Although now would be the perfect time to have a fling or two, don't you agree? I mean, there's hardly any danger in it anymore, is there? I can't get more pregnant than I already am." And with that she stomped out of the garage.

CHAPTER EIGHT

Chase followed Jo into the kitchen, his expression letting her know that facing her family had been child's play compared to facing her angry neighbor.

"Just what the hell was that remark supposed to mean?" he asked roughly, his arms folded aggressively across his chest. There was nothing gentle or understanding about him at that moment, Jo thought as she met his glacial stare.

"I was merely telling you what I assumed you wanted to hear," she explained. "You're the one always ready to jump to the worst conclusions where I'm concerned."

"I certainly didn't think you were out at any damn singles' bar," Chase snapped. "But it is after eleven o'clock, and in case you didn't know it, Ms. Benoit, a woman on a motor scooter at night isn't the safest thing in the world."

"True," she was forced to admit. "But do we have to fight about it?" she asked over her shoulder while she got down a glass, opened the fridge, and poured herself a glass of milk. "I'll start looking for a car tomorrow. Will that make you happy?"

"Not until I see you in it."

"If you're that worried, then why don't you find one that I can afford?" she suggested hopefully.

"Exactly what can you afford?" Chase jumped on the question. At least he could get that worry off his mind. Already he'd found a couple of nice used cars that he thought would be the very thing for her. Frankly, he would have preferred a new model, but he wasn't privy to Jo's finances, and he was positive she wouldn't accept help from him.

Jo named a figure that she felt certain was going to bankrupt her, but under the circumstances there was little she could do about it. It just meant that instead of going away for a week in September as she'd planned, she would be hard at work on the illustrations for a book she'd already said she couldn't do.

"You do believe in miracles, don't you?" Chase muttered sarcastically, his gaze lingering on the gentle thrust of her breasts beneath the pink silk blouse she was wearing. Stop it! an annoying little voice prodded him. This is a pregnant woman, for crying out loud. She is definitely not a candidate for the type of meaningless affairs you indulge in.

"Don't you think we can find something in that price range?" Jo frowned.

"Sure. At that price, we might be able to hook a sidecar on the scooter."

Jo forced herself to meet his gaze, wondering why she was finding it more and more difficult to relax in this man's presence. For months she'd heard about Chase from Bink. She'd been told things about him that, though certainly not unmentionable, were rather personal. Since actually meeting him, he'd run the gamit of emotions with her, from mistrust to anger. But above all else, he'd shown her kindness and concern for her welfare. Caution warned her, however, not to make more of his concern than it really was. She was alone and pregnant. Without those two factors, he probably wouldn't give her the time of day.

"How about a cup of coffee?" she asked, hoping the slight tremble in her voice wasn't noticed.

"All right."

As she put the coffee on to make, Jo found herself wondering how Chase had spent his evening. He was certainly dressed for something other than a drop-in visit next door, and somehow that didn't please her. The jacket of the lightweight, dark-gray suit hugged the outline of his shoulders as if it had been tailored for him. But then, she thought with a shrug, why shouldn't Chase Colbern wear tailored suits? Colbern Engineers was a worldwide firm with an excellent reputation, and Chase was part owner.

When Jo joined Chase at the table, the bland

expression on her face bore no hint of the thoughts buzzing around in her head. Chase was a free and single man, wasn't he? There was no reason why his activities for the evening should interest her.

"Did you have a nice evening?" The words popped effortlessly from Jo's mouth, leaving her to wonder how it was possible for a person to be so firmly convinced of one train of thought, then turn around and voice the opposite.

"It was pleasant enough," Chase replied. "I had dinner with an old friend I hadn't seen in several months. And you?" His gaze touched on every available inch of her that was visible. "Neat and tidy" kept running through his mind. A tiny slip of femininity that had entered his life and refused to be cast aside.

"Dinner at my parents. I told them about the baby." Jo made no effort to elaborate on her evening, her mind involved with other things. She was imagining Chase escorting a tall, beautiful woman to dinner. Had they been lovers at one time? Were they still?

"How did they take it?"

"Who?" She looked at him, puzzled.

"Your family." He sighed, as he began his usual round-about way with Jo of trying to get an answer. "What was their reaction when you told them you were pregnant?"

"Oh—yes." She sobered. "Better than I thought it would be. They were only in shock for a few minutes rather than days. They were also quite relieved when they found out Lance was the father."

"You told them everything?" Chase asked curiously.

"No. The only reason I mentioned Lance was so that they wouldn't panic thinking I'd gotten caught sleeping around," she answered matter-of-factly. "I didn't go into the details. What happened with Lance was private, something I've tried to put out of my mind. I don't want them barging into my life," she said frankly. "I've managed quite nicely without them, and I won't tolerate any interference from them at this stage."

"That shouldn't be a problem." He gave her a rakish grin. "You seem to have a knack for getting your way with most people."

Jo blushed. "You make me sound like a scheming female."

"Oh, you're definitely female, Ms. Benoit, but I would never call you scheming," he told her softly. "I just think you go about life a little differently from most people."

"Thank you for not saying I'm a kook. I've been called that on a number of occasions." Suddenly the conversation was too personal, Jo decided. There was something about Chase that always left her with the most peculiar longings. She couldn't decide if it was simply that he was a very attractive man, or if she was silly enough to actually entertain some wild notion that his attention stemmed from something deeper than his concern for a neighbor. Unfortunately, her pregnancy effectively put the skids to any plans she might have regarding Chase. What single, very eligible bachelor would want to be seen with a woman who resembled a whale?—which is exactly what she would look like in a few more months.

After drinking his coffee, Chase got up to leave. Jo followed him to the door, unaware of how forlorn she looked. "For the last fifteen minutes or so you've been looking as if you've lost your best friend," he said softly, smiling down at her. "Is something troubling you?" For some reason he wanted to know if she had decided to keep the baby. It was certainly none of his business, but somehow he felt that if Jo gave her baby up for adoption, she would always regret it.

"Just thinking of the months to come."

"Then don't think about them. Take each day as it comes." He reached out and cupped his palm to the back of her neck, then bent and kissed her on the forehead, the skin beneath his lips soft and warm. "I'll pick you up tomorrow after lunch to go and look at some cars. Okay?"

"Okay."

Pulling the door closed behind him, Chase paused for a moment. He didn't want to leave her. Don't be an ass, he silently cursed himself. Think of that gorgeous redhead you had dinner with. Now *that*'s a woman. She's just waiting for you to say the word, and you could have an affair that would be pleasing for both of you. Besides, there aren't any of the problems connected with the lovely Rita that plague your charming neighbor.

He gave a quick shake of his head and walked on toward his own house. Rita offered nothing but a good time. And that's what he wanted, wasn't it? A good time with no responsibility.

He let himself into the large den where Jake had left a single lamp on. For some reason, he found himself looking at the future, his future, and seeing nothing but a succession of redheads or blondes or brunettes. All having gorgeous bodies, and no identities. They would bring him momentary pleasure, but what else? He tried to argue against the bleakness of that thought. He had a full life. There was Bink—and Jake. There was his family, and the firm, of which he was an important part. He almost nodded; things had never looked better.

"This is not the one I had in mind for you." Chase walked around the red VW, eyeing it as though it were a scab on the world. "It's not much safer than that damn scooter you ride."

"It's cute," Jo quickly defended the little car. It was now almost three hours since they'd left her house, three hours during which she'd been in and out of a dozen or more cars. None of them had appealed to her until she saw this one. She turned

113

to the salesman and smiled brightly. "Will it be all right if I drive it for a few blocks?"

"Yes, ma'am," the short, stocky man agreed, trying to ignore the blazing heat of Chase's gaze that was pinned on him. "Er—but I think your husband is right, ma'am. That little blue car over there would probably be better for you."

"The 'little blue one' doesn't have personality," Jo said briskly. "And the gentleman is not my husband."

"Oh—oh, in that case . . ." He gave Chase a defeated shrug of the shoulders and reluctantly handed over the keys.

Jo opened the door and eased herself behind the wheel. Before she could get the key into the ignition though, Chase was climbing into the passenger seat—which took some doing, considering his size and the amount of space allotted him.

"It really isn't necessary for you to come along," she told him quietly. One would have thought she was out to buy the Hope diamond from the way he had dragged her from one dealership to the other. At the moment, she was hot and tired and ready to settle for a donkey. Which was exactly what she was beginning to think she had seated next to her.

"I beg to differ, Ms. Benoit," Chase said with a growl. "This is the first car we've tried without an automatic transmission. I'll be damned if I'll put my stamp of approval on something that will get you killed."

114

The "Ms. Benoit" meant he was annoyed with her, again, Jo thought with a sigh. She'd also noticed that for such a large, commanding person, he certainly spent a lot of his time grinding his teeth. "Don't worry, Chase, I can take care of myself."

"That's a crock, and we both know it." He dismissed her independent stand without batting an eye. "Shall we go?" he further infuriated her by asking.

Jo started the engine, then grabbed the gear stick and slammed it down into first, determined to show him that she knew what she was doing. She let out on the clutch and pressed on the gas. The VW shot forward like a bat out of hell, the sudden forward motion almost sending her and Chase through the windshield. Oops! That was a bad move. Now he would think her incompetent. She made the turn into the slow lane of traffic on two wheels, shifted into second and passed one car before slamming into third gear and slowing down.

A quick glance at Chase showed him not to be the least bit shaken by her mistake or impressed at how well she had handled it. In fact, he was calmly leafing through a small book that listed the recommended price for automobiles. "Would you mind seeing if the air conditioning works?" she asked.

"My pleasure," he snapped. Jo winced as he jabbed and jerked at the lever and buttons. When the burst of cold hit them, she smiled.

"Thank you. That feels nice." After driving on

for a few minutes, she looked at a scowling Chase. "I think this is the one."

"May I ask exactly what it is about this tin can that appeals to you?"

"It's red—"

"And that makes it okay?" he asked incredulously.

"You didn't let me finish." She frowned. "It—it also feels right. I can tell that we will get along well."

"How about the engine? The number of miles? The condition of the tires?" he rattled off. "Have you considered any of the above at all?"

"Isn't that what you were doing when you and Mr.—er—what's his name were huddled beneath the hood?"

"Well, somebody had to do it." Chase seemed eager to impart this bit of news to her. "You don't buy a car like you would a cake in a bakery."

Jo digested that bit of information, then nodded. "You're right. Those things definitely do need considering."

"Well, thank you, Ms. Benoit," he retorted sourly.

"It's not going so well, is it?"

Chase turned his head and listened. The engine seemed all right to him. "What doesn't seem to be going well?" Damn screwy woman. He should have known better than to get involved with her.

"The desk."

"The desk," he repeated to himself in a questioning undertone.

"You being tied to a desk, Chase," Jo explained. "You told me yourself that you weren't looking forward to it. For the last three days you've been stalking around with a murderous gleam in your eye. I think even Bink is wishing you would take a vacation."

"I'll adjust," he said after a few moments of silence. "Bink needs me now."

"Of course he does," Jo agreed, though the index and middle finger of both hands were crossed. Bink needed a father, not Attila the Hun charging about. "Bink's a nice boy. He's always doing something for me. I'll have to make him some cookies," she said decisively.

"Oh—er—you shouldn't tire yourself out cooking over a hot stove." Chase was quick to discourage her, remembering how sick of oatmeal cookies Bink was getting.

"Nonsense, it's no bother. Besides, I need an excuse to visit Jake."

"You don't need an excuse to visit Jake," Chase remarked ruefully. "He's already your willing slave."

"That's nice," Jo commented softly as she drove the car into the dealership lot. "I hope he'll feel that way when I ask him to be my partner in the natural childbirth classes I plan to attend." She opened the door and stepped out, smiling at the waiting salesman. "I'll take it."

Chase sat as though thunderstruck. She really hadn't said that, had she? But he knew he hadn't suddenly developed a hearing problem. Good God! His mind boggled at the scene he conjured up of Jake in a roomful of pregnant women. With a lightness of step that hadn't been there before trying out the VW, he left the car, flashed the startled salesman a satisfied grin, then got down to the nuts and bolts of a genuine bit of horse tradin'.

CHAPTER NINE

"Make the usual number of copies of that memo, Laura, and make sure my dad gets one. I think that should just about do it. Oh, and Laura." He frowned at his desk calendar. "What's this lunch date tomorrow with C. Frame?"

"That's the man you wanted to talk to about those new drills, Chase," Laura Channing explained. She'd worked for Colbern Engineering for over fifteen years as secretary to Matthew Colbern and was filling in for Chase now until a suitable secretary could be found for him.

"Ah yes." He frowned. "I don't suppose Brent or Simon could see him?"

"They could, but I'm sure they'd much rather you made the decision. So would your dad, for that matter."

"Why do I get the idea that I'm being slowly wrapped in baling wire so that I can't escape this place?" Chase stared pointedly at the attractive older woman.

She chuckled. "Don't take it so hard. Your dad

has been patient all these years while you wandered over the world."

"Wandered, hell!" Chase exclaimed. He got to his feet and walked to the large window of his office and looked out. For mile after mile there was nothing but concrete and glass. He couldn't even see a bird flying. He turned and stared at Laura. "I've worked damn hard. I never once played and let the business suffer."

"Everyone knows that, Chase," Laura said soothingly. "Without your expert eye on several government projects, this company could have lost its shirt. Instead we're at the top of the heap now. In the first three months of this year alone, we turned down five jobs. That's quite an accomplishment, Chase."

"Yeah, I guess it is."

Laura started toward the door just as Matthew Colbern opened it and walked in. He caught Laura's warning look and his son's agitated prowling about the office in one brief glance. "So the natives are restless, eh?"

Laura smiled and closed the door behind. Chase gave his dad a wary look, then waved him to a chair. "What's on your mind?"

"Just a social call, Chase," the elder Colbern spoke casually as he sat down. "Your brothers were afraid to brave the lion in his den, so I was nominated."

Chase looked embarrassed for a moment, then

grinned. "I suppose I haven't been the easiest person to get along with these last few days."

"That's putting it mildly. Is there some problem I need to know about?"

"Could you possibly transform this cell into a stretch of hot, arid land, with a moon and a sprinkling of stars at night?" Chase scowled as he dropped into his chair behind the massive desk.

"I'm afraid that is one thing I can't do," Matthew said with a sigh. "I can, however, point out the advantages of having you here, starting with the tremendous amount of work you've taken off me. Having you here with me has even gotten me to start thinking of retiring."

"You? Retire?" Chase said jokingly. "That'll be the day."

"Is that what you really think?"

"Of course it is. You *are* Colbern Engineering, Dad. You started this company on a shoestring. You weathered some tough years in order to keep it a family concern. Retirement." He shook his head. "We'll probably have to make an appointment with you to bury you, you old coot."

"Correction, Chase," Matthew returned without the slightest rancor. "I *was* Colbern Engineering, until you became the company watch dog. You'd be surprised at the number of contracts we've obtained simply by agreeing that you would head up the project. I must admit to a sense of pride, son, at the way you've handled yourself. And," he went on, "when I retire you will take over the reins of the company."

Chase could feel the noose tightening around his neck. He gave his father a quick, thorough once over. "You aren't sick or something, are you?"

"No." Matthew smiled at him. "I feel fine."

"Good." A burst of relief sounded from Chase. "For a moment there you had me worried."

"But I am planning on retiring in six months."

It was close to six o'clock when Chase wheeled into the driveway of his home, his expression one of suppressed fury. Damn it to hell! He would resign. There was no way he was going to let his father tie him to that damn company for the rest of his life. But somewhere in the back of his mind, even as he ranted and raved, Chase could see the bars of the proper life-style of an executive slowly closing in on him. On the other side of the bars was freedom, the right to come and go as he pleased, the pleasure of walking outside in the middle of the night, if he chose, without seeing another single human being.

He opened the door and stalked into the kitchen, where Jake was just taking a roast out of the oven. Without speaking, Chase banged his briefcase onto the bar, then walked determinedly to the cupboard where the liquor was kept and fixed himself a scotch.

He turned, half expecting to find Jake glaring at

him. But Jake seemed too preoccupied with his own problems to worry about anyone else. As Chase let his gaze slowly travel about the kitchen, he saw a plate of neatly wrapped oatmeal cookies setting on the counter. Ah-ha, he thought merrily, his own troubles forgotten, it looked as though Ms. Benoit had indeed visited.

"How did your day go, Jake?"

"Hurmph!"

"Is that a good, bad, or indifferent hurmph?" Chase asked smoothly.

"I haven't decided yet," Jake said with a growl. He placed the roast back into the oven, then stirred the contents of a saucepan on the stove.

Chase walked over and fingered the plastic wrap covering the cookies. "Looks like our neighbor has been over. Did you have a nice visit?"

"Good enough," Jake snapped. He turned and fixed Chase with a quelling stare. "I don't think I've ever been caught in a more difficult situation."

"Oh?"

"Jo asked me if I would attend natural childbirth classes with her as her partner. What do you think of that?"

"Well"—Chase struggled not to laugh—"I understand the partner plays a very important role. I should think you would be honored that she asked you."

"I am." Jake looked so harassed Chase was tempted to reach out and pat him. "It's just that—" He waved both hands in an attempt to express himself. "I don't think I could see her through to the end, Chase. Having a baby is a damn gory process."

"Have you ever seen a baby being born?"

"Hell, no." Jake spluttered. "I'm not very handy when it comes to things like that. Besides, I care a lot for Jo, and I don't think I could stand seeing her in pain."

"Buck up, Jake." Chase did pat him on the shoulder then. "Once you get involved, I'm sure the rest will be smooth sailing. Just think, if it's a boy she might name it after you."

"You think this is all very amusing, don't you?" Jake glared at him.

"Certainly not," Chase lied with a perfectly straight face. "I think Jo is paying you a very nice compliment. She probably sees you as a father figure, someone who's courageous and strong. That's the type of individual she will need to help her through this pregnancy."

"It's a crying shame she can't call on her own father or brothers."

"According to what she's told me, I seriously doubt any of them would do. She's not that close to her dad, and her brothers seem to be pretty cold fish. Don't worry, you'll make out just fine."

During dinner Bink surprised Jake and Chase by asking when Jo was expecting her baby.

"How did you know she was pregnant?" Chase

carefully probed after a quick look at Jake, to which the latter shrugged and shook his head.

"Simple," his son admitted openly. "I listened to you and Jake discussing it. I think her husband Lance was a rat, and I hope Jo keeps the baby. It will be kind of neat having a little kid around." He looked thoughtful for a moment. "Does this mean I'll have to keep on mowing her grass and taking out her garbage?"

"Would you mind?" Chase asked.

"Naa—I guess not," Bink gave in reluctantly. "But it looks to me like it would solve a lot of problems for all of us if she just moved in here. We've got plenty of room."

Jake became very involved with the food on his plate, his lips twitching suspiciously. Chase struggled not to embarrass his son, but at the same time he had to point out that his suggestion wasn't feasible. "Jo's a pretty independent lady, son. Besides, it wouldn't look right for her to live with us. This is an all-male household, and people might get the wrong idea."

"I suppose you're right," Bink conceded, "but I still think it's dumb. Will you be helping her get the nursery fixed up?" he asked his father.

"How do you know she's ready to start the nursery?"

"I was over there awhile ago, and I heard her talking to Mo. He says he's pretty handy with a hammer and saw, but Jo told me she really doesn't

125

think he knows anything about carpentry. I told her that you were really good at building things and that you would help her."

"Perhaps we should wait and see if she wants our help, Bink. After all, we can't simply walk in and take over."

"Aw, Dad," Bink wailed. "Jo's like family."

"I agree with Bink," Jake said, favoring Chase with a facetious grin. "She's all alone right now and needs her friends rallying around her."

"I've rallied," Chase replied coolly. "I finally got her off that damn scooter and into a car. I would also like to eat one meal in this house without having to hear a running account of Jo and her problems."

Neither Bink nor Jake commented on that remark. Rather, they ignored Chase for the rest of the meal.

Later that evening, after everyone was in bed and the house was quiet, Chase pushed back from the desk where he'd been looking over some work he'd brought home from the office. He was restless. He looked at his watch, surprised to see that it was almost midnight. He raised his arms over his head and stretched. Maybe another drink before bed, he thought, then vetoed that idea. Jake was right, he was drinking too much, and all it was giving him was a very bad headache in the mornings.

With a disgusted look on his face, he got up and walked through the silent house out to the patio.

Perhaps a few minutes outside would help him relax. But as he went to sit down, Chase glanced toward Jo's house. "What the hell?" he muttered beneath his breath, then went charging across the yard to her back door and rapped his knuckles in a demanding knock.

It took several minutes before the object of his anger appeared, and when she did, Chase's mouth was in full stride.

"Will you please tell me what you think you are doing standing on a ladder at midnight?" he asked the moment Jo opened the door. He pushed by her to the center of the kitchen, then whirled about and faced her, his expression ominous.

Jo tipped back her head, her hair covered with a blue and white cotton kerchief, a smear of yellow paint on her cheek. She calmly regarded him for several seconds. "I agree with your mother," she said simply.

Chase blinked several times in rapid succession, wondering what the flaming hell she was talking about. He was also acutely aware, to his chagrin, of the brevity of the shorts and halter she was wearing. How the hell was it possible for him to be getting the most painful urges to make love to Jo Benoit when he knew she was pregnant? What was happening to his sense of decency? he asked himself. Why, his palms were even sweaty! "What has my mother got to do with anything?" he croaked

127

like a huge bullfrog ready to pounce on an unsuspecting insect.

"She thinks, and I agree, that your blood pressure must be sky high these days. Have you had it checked lately?"

"Kindly leave my mother and my blood pressure out of this discussion." Damn it! His voice still sounded peculiar. "The reason for my being here has to do with walking out onto my patio and seeing you, through an open window, standing on a stepladder."

"I was painting." Jo smiled. "Would you like to see what I've done so far?" Without waiting, she grabbed him by the hand and pulled him after her. An electric shock shot through Chase's body the instant he felt her touch. He knew it wasn't lightning, he reasoned dazedly, because there hadn't been a single cloud in the sky when he was out. He wrenched his hand from Jo's grip the moment they entered the room and plunged it into his pants pocket.

Jo stood beside him and waved a small hand toward part of one wall, painted a soft shade of yellow. "What do you think? If you were a baby, would you like that particular shade?"

"It's very nice."

"Mmmm. Stiff."

"I beg your pardon?"

"Your voice, it's stiff."

"But the color is nice. Isn't that what we're suppose to be discussing?"

"True. But an 'It's nice' given grudgingly isn't exactly what I had in mind when I asked your opinion."

"It's beautiful! If I were a baby sleeping in this room, I'd wake up each morning warbling like a bird because of the softness, the warmth of the color. Does that suit you better?"

"Much."

"Is my opinion very important?"

"Very."

"Why?"

"When I find out myself, I'll be sure to tell you."

Chase stared down into the velvet gray of her eyes, his heart leaping to his throat. Somehow during the conversation his hands had found their way to Jo's shoulders and his fingers were slowly caressing the softness of her skin. She stood small and defenseless beneath his touch, and he felt drugged. Doped. He felt like a first-class fool. His tongue was coming unhinged and wouldn't obey his brain. "I'm sorry for barging in on you like some idiot, but you frightened the hell out of me when I saw you on that ladder," he murmured. Only inches separated them, and at the slightest pressure of his hands, he felt the tips of her breasts pressing against his chest.

Jo was tongue-tied. The immenseness of Chase seemed to fill the room, and the spicy fragrance she'd come to associate with him was all around her. Her eyes were pinpointed on his lips, and for the life of her she couldn't move. Soft undulating ripples of pleasure were pulsing throughout her body, and she was terribly afraid she was about to make a complete fool of herself. She felt the gentle pressure of Chase's hands edge her closer. She saw the sensual fullness of his lips pass before her eyes, then felt their lingering touch against her mouth.

Her hands went up instinctively to his shoulders, her body straining on tiptoe so that her fingertips could twine themselves in the rough edges of hair that grew on his neck. His tongue was like a hot, flaming tip, touching, then darting one after another sensitive points of her mouth. Jo heard a soft sigh of pleasure burst into their midst and was surprised when she realized that it came from her.

Chase's hands slipped from her shoulders and made long, tantalizingly slow sweeps from the gentle swell of her hips to her shoulders. The motion reminded Jo of the slow building of a wave as it slipped effortlessly along till the crest gathered itself together, rose, and then was swept away only to begin all over again.

That was what Chase was doing to her, and it seemed the most wonderful and natural thing in the world, Jo thought in the hazy fog of contentment surrounding her. His hands were giant waves, and her body was the piece of driftwood, waiting to be honed and nurtured by the ocean.

Suddenly the hands on her body stilled. The warmth and desire steadily encroaching upon her mind halted. Jo opened her eyes, clouded with the ecstasy of the moment.

She saw a stern-faced Chase. His lips, only seconds ago creating a wealth of tenderness, now resembled two bold slashes across his face. Again her shoulders were gripped and she was moved back gently but firmly.

"I'm sorry, Jo." She saw his lips move and heard the words. But it was a moment before she could respond.

"Why?" She blinked in an attempt to clear her head. Why on earth was he apologizing?

"It was a thoughtless thing for me to do," Chase muttered. "For a moment I forgot." He dropped his hands and turned away from her.

"I enjoyed it—very much. From the way your heart was pounding, I think you did too. Why did you suddenly pull away and look embarrassed?"

Chase looked at her over his shoulder, his gaze sweeping her from head to toe. "You're pregnant, for Christ's sake!"

"I know." Jo nodded slowly. "But I'm not dead. Being pregnant hasn't dried up my libido, you know."

Chase swung around and faced her. "How can you talk like that?"

"We shared a kiss, Chase, we didn't make love. If we had, I'm sure I'd have enjoyed that even

131

more," she stated boldly, suppressing the mischievous twinkle in her eyes.

An expression of total frustration slipped over his face. "Are you this frank with all the men you go out with?" he asked hoarsely.

"So far, you're the first. I'll let you know after tomorrow evening. I'm having dinner with Harry."

"Who the hell is Harry?"

"Handsome Harry, as he's called behind his back by some of us who know him, is in advertising. Mary Clare, Carla, and I are hoping he can be persuaded to come up with an ad campaign that will help the sale of our greeting cards but won't cost us his usual fortune."

"Let Mary Clare or Carla be the bait," Chase bit out viciously. The fact that Jo would even think of dating hit him right between the eyes. Why, she should be home, knitting or whatever it was that a pregnant woman did while she waited for her baby to be born.

"I don't knit."

Chase glowered suspiciously. "How the hell did you know what I was thinking?"

"It's a gift." She smiled innocently. "Are you as good a carpenter as Bink says you are?"

CHAPTER TEN

Chase let his fingers trail along the smooth skin of one gleaming shoulder as he kissed the pouting mouth that opened so readily. Long, red-tipped fingers worked their way through the front of his shirt and were caressing his hair-coarsened chest.

"Oh, Chase," the dewy-eyed blonde whispered as she eased her head back against his arm and smiled up at him. "I've missed you. I've missed your arms around me, I've missed your kisses, but most of all, I've missed having you make love to me. Why don't we adjourn this very exciting reunion to the bedroom, hmmm?"

Without being aware of it a certain indifference had edged its way into Chase's hooded gaze. For most of the evening, peculiar flashbacks had haunted him. And it wasn't the first time either. No matter which woman he was with, his mind wouldn't let go of Jo. He saw her in every small, dark-haired woman that crossed his path. He felt her presence with him from the dimly lit restaurants and clubs to the cozy late-night moments he spent with his various dates. In short, he thought disgustedly, he couldn't escape that gray-eyed witch, and it was beginning to get on his nerves.

His sex life was zilch! He hadn't gone to bed with a woman in months, and he blamed it all on Jo Benoit.

"Chase?" Lola Raynard wiggled in his arms, pressing her ample breasts against his chest in a seductive maneuver that normally would have set him on fire. "My bedroom, remember?" she whispered huskily.

Chase remembered, all right. And for a moment he almost found the urge to pick her up in his arms and discover all the delightful talents Lola was so willing to impart. He cursed himself. He cursed the world in general. He was going crazy. That was it, he told himself. He was going stark raving mad. He looked at the long, slender body sprawled across his thighs and realized there wasn't the slightest bit of desire for her racing through his body as it should have been—as it would have been a few months ago. Instead of seeing Lola's very definite charms, he saw a tiny, plump figure with a heart-shaped face and dark hair.

With no thought for his actions, Chase pushed the bewildered beauty from his lap and came to his feet. His lips twisted ruefully. "Sorry, Lola," he muttered as he pulled his shirt back in place, "I just remembered someone I'm supposed to call."

"At ten o'clock in the evening?" she cried out in disbelief.

"Mmmm." He evaded the question, then reached for his jacket and headed for the door.

"Chase," the sexy blonde wailed as she sprung to her feet and hurried after him. "What's wrong? Was it something I did or didn't do?"

"No, no," he hastily assured her, even dropping a light kiss on her startled mouth. "I'm really pushed for time these days. What with adjusting to the office, looking after Bink—you know how it is." The words rushed from his mouth in a hurried spate. "See you around."

When he got to his car, he sat behind the wheel for several minutes, so infuriated with himself he wasn't sure he could drive. Damnation! he swore. He was single and eligible as hell. So why didn't he stay and make Lola's dreams for the evening come true? He could still go back. Why didn't he? He couldn't let all those pleasant moments go to waste. They were his for the taking. But the pep talk didn't work. Nothing was going to work, Chase told himself, not until he got out of this damned relationship with Jo.

All the way home he berated himself, cursed his stupidity. There was no way in this world he could actually care for Jo Benoit. No way at all. But the entire time he was reminding himself of this fact, he was wondering if she was all right. He knew for a fact she had a doctor's appointment tomorrow, because he'd marked it down on his calendar. Which was a stupid thing to do, he told himself sternly. But in months past, Jo had been known to forget such important things.

And you think it's your place to remind her? the irritating voice that had been badgering him asked. Well, who the hell else is going to look after her? Chase argued silently. Her family is an uncaring bunch of bastards, and she can wrap her friends around her finger. Somebody has to be firm with her.

Does the lady in question know that you love her?

Chase slammed on the brakes of his powerful Mercedes, almost causing a five-car pileup behind him. Damn it all, he was not in love with Jo Benoit! Why, he'd only kissed the infuriating little witch one time. But the longer he fought against the idea, the more convinced he became that it was true. And with each second of realization came a wave of bone-chilling fear.

Jo stared thoughtfully at the second in a four-part series of ad campaigns set up for Personal Touch Greeting Cards.

"The first ad has been out now for over three months. I think it's time to change over to this one." Harry Mullins pointed to the second layout that was being looked over.

"I like it." Mary Clare nodded.

"So do I," shy, retiring Carla agreed.

"Make it three." Jo smiled at Harry. "It's not pushy, yet it still makes one aware of the product."

"My intentions exactly," Harry said proudly. "Well, now that that's settled, why don't we go somewhere for dinner? It's not often that I get the chance to work with three such agreeable ladies."

"Aren't we supposed to wait for Mo?" Jo asked Mary Clare.

"Oh, yes." The blonde grimaced. "I'd forgotten."

Jo and Carla exchanged amused glances. Mo Tyson and Mary Clare were at each other constantly. Jo was convinced that if her stubborn partner would give Mo half a chance, he could make her very happy. Mary Clare's past had been riddled with unfaithful men, including an ex-husband who had not only left her for another woman, but had cleaned out their savings as well. Now she viewed every man she met with suspicion, and poor Mo was no exception.

"Why don't we all go over to my place?" Jo asked. "We can decide on dinner and call in our order. How does Chinese sound? You wouldn't mind picking it up, would you, Harry? Besides," she added for extra leverage, "I'm a little tired."

Immediately all eyes turned to her and her bulging tummy; concern showed on her friends' faces. "Lord!" Mary Clare rolled her eyes. "If we bring you home sick, Chase will have my head. I promised him I wouldn't let you overdo it."

Jo merely smiled at the mention of her neighbor, then led the way out of the office. During the drive to her house in Mary Clare's car, with Harry following them, she was content to sit and listen to Mary Clare and Carla argue back and forth about the pros and cons of adding special orders of Christmas cards to the line. Privately Jo thought the idea a good one, but she wasn't in the mood to debate the issue. There would be enough time for that later on. Her thoughts were on Chase and the uncanny way he'd managed to move into her life during the past several months.

She glanced down at her protruding stomach and winced. Only eight more weeks to go. In her mind she tried to envision herself slim once more, opening the door to a smiling, sexy Chase and having him sweep her into his arms. But somehow her mind wouldn't cooperate, and all she could see was herself, forever pregnant, while Chase flitted from one long-legged beauty to another. Suddenly she knew she hated all women over five feet two, with slim bodies and full breasts. The only time she'd ever had any bosom to speak of was now, which was very cruel, considering the rest of her figure had gone to hell and back. It wasn't fair—wasn't fair at all.

In her mind she went back over each time Chase had touched her. After that evening when he'd kissed her, he'd gone out of his way for days to avoid any physical contact between them. At first this had amused Jo, but then it had become irritating. He acted as though being pregnant automatically carried with it the vow of celibacy. Not that she was interested in an affair, Jo reasoned. That was the furthest thing from her mind. But she didn't like being automatically dismissed as unattractive or, worse still, as having not the tiniest flicker of desire for the male sex. She was quite certain that once the baby was born, she would want a fuller life in every sense. Would Chase be the man she would share that life with?

She thought of the untold moments he'd spent with her—seeing that she exercised regularly, even to walking a mile or more with her in the late evening. He'd bought almost every book on the market that dealt with child care. That had really amused Jo.

"Aren't you afraid someone will think you slightly off your rocker if they see you buying this type of literature?" she'd asked him as she thumbed through his latest find.

"It's none of their damned business," Chase had retorted, scowling at her. He'd reached out and plucked the book from her hands and begun dragging her toward the door. "Come on, pudgy," he teased, knowing she hated the name. "It's time for your walk. Did you take your vitamins today?"

"It's too early for a walk," Jo had argued. "I'll go later when it cools off some."

"Oh, no you don't," her eagle-eyed warden had vetoed that idea. "The last time I fell for that line, you didn't get any exercise to speak of for almost a week."

"I know." Jo had sighed. "It was heavenly. And to answer your other question—yes, I took the vitamins. They upset my stomach. Do you have a sure-fire remedy for that little problem, Mr. Fix-it?"

Even the preparation of the nursery hadn't escaped his attention. He'd completely redesigned the closet, adding one row of drawers from floor to ceiling, rearranging the shelves and the clothes rod. There had been times in the past months when Jo wondered if his apparent excitement over the baby was due in part to the fact that he'd been separated from Bink's mother during most of her pregnancy. She hadn't pried, but from what Chase let slip from time to time, she'd gotten the impression that he was unconsciously reliving a time in his life that had been denied him.

She also learned that Chase Colbern, for all his bluff and bluster, was a very gentle man. She'd seen him angry and she'd seen him brimming with laughter. Such as the time when he was helping her clean out the closet in the nursery.

"Judas Priest!" he'd exclaimed, holding up a contraption of wires, springs, and hand grips.

"What the hell is this? And this?" He hooted, discovering two more innocent-looking articles that had sworn to give her a thirty-six-inch bust in just days.

"I'll thank you not to go plundering through my things!" Jo said testily as she snatched his find from his large hands. She promptly stuffed the offending monster into the garbage bag, her face red as a beet.

"Don't tell me you actually paid money for that crap?" he asked disbelievingly.

"I certainly did," she replied stiffly. "What's it to you?"

"Did it work?" he had the audacity to ask, his eyes glowing with amusement as he surveyed her tiny, plump figure.

"That's a low blow, and you know it. I'm as flat-chested as a flounder, you swine."

Chase cocked his head to one side and critically regarded her full breasts. "You definitely wouldn't pass for a flounder now, Ms. Benoit," he gleefully informed her.

"Stick it in your ear!" Jo glared at him, turning on her heel and marching from the room. She refused to speak to him for nearly an hour, but Chase was persistent. He disappeared for a short time, then returned with two triple banana splits. Jo wasn't dumb. She knew when to wage war and when to give in.

But now, she told herself, there were only approximately two months left. What would happen when the baby was born? Would Chase drop her and go his merry way? Somehow, just the thought of that made the future look bleak and lonely.

And that's the silliest thing you've ever done, pinning your hopes on that man, she told herself wearily. Chase looks upon you as an object of pity. Don't misconstrue the attention he's giving you now for anything but what it is—concern and consideration for a woman alone. Besides, by the time the baby is born, Chase will probably have had enough of being tied to a desk. One morning you'll wake up and find he's taken off for Pago Pago or some other ridiculous place.

Moments later, when they were getting out of the car in Jo's driveway, Mary Clare looked over toward Chase's. "I see your handsome neighbor is out this evening. Did I tell you that I ran into him a couple of nights ago at Freddy's?" she asked Jo. "He was with some redhead, dripping with diamonds."

"That was 'Fabulous Rita,'" Jo remarked offhandedly as she led the way into the kitchen.

"Have you met her?" Mary Clare asked curiously.

"Once when she dropped in unexpectedly on Chase. He was over here working on the nursery. If you think she's something, you should see the blond bombshell Lola. I'm convinced her bosom

142

precedes her by at least five minutes before she enters a room."

"Jealous?"

"Insanely so." Jo sighed. "As you two well know, I've spent a fortune on different ways to increase my bust size."

"You certainly picked a winner this last time." Quiet Carla spoke up, eyeing Jo's belly. Jo and Mary Clare stared at their shy, unassuming partner, then burst out laughing. When Harry entered moments later, he thought they'd all gone nuts.

"May I share the joke?" He looked at each of them expectantly.

"No," Mary Clare said sternly. "All we want out of you is dinner." She told Jo to sit down and prop up her feet, then whipped out a pencil and pad and took down each order for dinner. She handed the slip of paper to Harry. "There's the phone." She nodded toward the wall phone by the fridge. "We're starving."

"Gee." Harry grinned, unruffled. "It's so nice to be needed. But shouldn't we wait for Mo?"

"I really—" Carla began, only to be interrupted by Mary Clare.

"I'm sure that behemoth has already eaten; it's almost eight-thirty. Besides, you have no idea what you would be getting into if you offered to feed Mo Tyson."

Harry placed the order, while Mary Clare and Carla made iced tea and set the table. "How about a few hands of bridge after we eat?" Harry suggested.

"Sounds like fun," Jo seconded. It would be fun, and it might help her rest better. Lately she'd had problems sleeping. It might also help keep your mind off Chase Colbern, a little voice whispered.

During dinner Jo got two phone calls. The first one was from her mother, who wanted to know if Jo was coming to dinner the next evening.

"I'm afraid not, Mom. I'm working on a pretty tight schedule, and by the time I get through, I'm bushed."

"Really, Jo," Sarah said coolly. "I should think having dinner with your family would be enjoyable. Nevertheless, if you won't come to us, I'll bring your dinner to you."

"That's sweet, Mom, but I couldn't let you do that. I'm perfectly capable of fixing my own food."

"Don't be silly, Jo," her mother scolded her. "That's my grandchild you're carrying, and I want to know that it's getting the proper nourishment." During those first two weeks immediately after she'd learned she was pregnant and was still not certain she wanted to keep the baby, Jo had gotten the distinct impression that her mother was all for her giving it up for adoption. But once Jo made up her mind to keep her baby, Sarah Kincaid had begun acting as though the idea had been hers alone.

After Jo was back at the table, Mary Clare made

the same observation. "I must say, I can't figure her out."

"Neither can I," Jo admitted.

"It's been said that very sane, normal people, even cold ones, have been known to act quite out of the ordinary at the birth of a grandchild," Carla said timidly. "Perhaps that's what is happening with your mother."

At this solemn prediction, Jo paled, remembering other stories of doting grandparents. She wondered fleetingly if she could afford to move to another city.

The next call was from Elise. "I just wanted you to know that I stumbled onto the most marvelous sale today at that cute little childrens' boutique," her sister said. "I'm afraid I lost all control and almost bought them out."

"How nice," Jo mumbled, a bit confused by her sister's unexpected enthusiasm. It wasn't like Elise at all.

"Do I hear voices?" Elise asked after describing to Jo several of the outfits she'd bought.

"Yes. I have some friends over, and we're just finishing dinner." Jo jumped at the chance to get off the phone.

After pointing out to Jo that it was quite late for an expectant mother to be eating dinner, Elise hung up.

Mo's arrival saved Carla the embarrassment of

having to be the fourth player at bridge, a game she was just learning.

Being with her friends gave Jo a much-needed diversion. She and Harry were partners against Mary Clare and Mo. The conversation was lively, thanks to the sparks constantly flying between Mary Clare and Mo. Jo caught the undercurrents of tension between them more than once and smiled to herself. Her blond friend had a sizable chip on her shoulder where men were concerned, but she had never come up against such an unflappable wall as Mo. He didn't cater to her every whim, or hang onto every word she spoke. In fact, Jo thought as she watched them arguing over a particular bid, her friend had finally met a man who wasn't impressed with her. It was causing Mary Clare some bad moments.

At the end of three games, Jo and Harry boasted loudly of their victory. Mary Clare shot arrows of exasperation toward Mo, who calmly ignored them. "Don't fret over losing, sweetie," he drawled in his loud voice. "With my expert coaching there's hope for you yet."

"How kind" was her frigid reply, her eyes like steely points. "I can hardly wait for the lessons to begin."

"Good. I'll be over at your place tomorrow evening no later than seven." Mo cooed like a giant bear, smiling at her as if his appearance at her door would be the highlight of her day.

Mary Clare bristled like a cat, while the others could barely contain their laughter. "Has it occurred to you, Mo Tyson, that I might have a date tomorrow evening?"

"Nonsense," he stated matter-of-factly while he returned the cards to the box and tidied up the table. "You're too contrary to have a date. You try your damnedest to scare off every man you meet. But not to worry," he told her calmly. "I've faced greater odds before and come out ahead."

Jo decided the moment had come when she should interrupt or be witness to Mary Clare leaping across the table and scratching Mo's eyes out. "Er—I hear they're having a sale on all their baby things at Dunbar's tomorrow." The arguing couple turned to stare at her as if inspecting a worm found in a salad. "Well"—she shrugged—"I just thought I'd try to keep you two from killing each other."

That broke the ice somewhat, and while her guests were walking to the door, Jo could have sworn she detected a rather pleased aura about Mary Clare.

The house was quiet after they'd gone. Jo walked through the silent rooms, her arms crossed over her breasts, her hands clasping her elbows. She'd had a nice, enjoyable evening, but she was still lonely. Why?

But the question was hardly necessary. The day had passed without her seeing Chase. Not even one little peek. His car had been gone when she got out of bed, and she had been away from home when he got off work. Silly, silly, she lectured herself. Why should he come over here, when he could be with Fabulous Rita?

She paused in the doorway of the nursery. Her soft gaze lingered over the tiny blue teddy bears and perky rabbits on the pale-yellow wallpaper that covered the wall where the crib would be. The other walls and trim were done in matching yellow. Carla, as handy with a needle as she was writing verse, had made fully lined curtains from material that matched the wallpaper. The only piece of furniture so far was a rosewood chest that had belonged to Jo's Grandmother Kincaid.

Standing in the quiet nursery, Jo wondered if the baby would feel the love the room seemed to radiate. Or would it know of her initial resentment? Jo turned and walked back down the hall to the kitchen. She hoped not. All the anguish and uncertainty she'd experienced when she'd learned she was pregnant was now harnessed into a wealth of love and an impatience for the day when she would hold her baby in her arms.

The thought of a cup of hot tea had just popped into her mind, when there was a knock on the back door. Jo hurried to answer it.

"Saw your company leaving just as I got home," Chase muttered as he stepped inside. "Isn't it a little late for you to be entertaining?"

148

Jo sniffed the air as he walked past her, her tiny nose quivering distastefully. "Lola," she said decisively, turning to face him. It was a sin, she thought resignedly, for a man to be as attractive as Chase. And the ironic thing about him was that he exuded sensuality as easily as most men breathed.

"I beg your pardon?" He frowned, his sharp gaze not missing the shadows beneath her eyes or the way she was holding her hands to the small of her back.

"That particular fragrance you're broadcasting," she said with a shrug, "is called Giorgio and sells for one hundred and fifty dollars an ounce. I always get a whiff of it when you've been out with Lola. I'd heard that Fabulous Rita had a penchant for diamonds, but I wasn't aware that Gorgeous Lola was also wealthy. Don't you ever date poor working girls?"

"Suppose we leave my preference for women out of this discussion." Chase turned away from her accusing eye. He walked on into the kitchen and began fixing himself a scotch and water. "Had your milk today?" he asked without looking up.

"No. I've sworn off the blasted stuff. It leaves my tongue coated."

Without another word, Chase got down a glass, opened the fridge, and filled the glass to the brim with milk. He handed it to Jo. "Drink," he ordered.

"Ugh," she muttered when the last drop was

downed, then popped the glass into the dishwasher. "This should be the healthiest kid in the world considering all the junk you make me swallow."

"The baby will be fine, and so will you," he said smoothly. He leaned against the edge of the counter and stared at her, his blue eyes warming as they ran over her. I love her, he told himself, somewhat awed by the admission. I love her. "Is your back bothering you?" he asked after a moment.

"Yes," Jo answered breathlessly. Having Chase stare at her was unnerving. What was he thinking? she wondered. Was he counting the days till he would be free of her? Was he hating himself for ever getting involved with her life?

"Turn around and rest your elbows on the counter," he told her. Jo looked puzzled, but did as she was told.

When the warmth of his hands slipped beneath the loose edge of her maternity smock and began to massage her back, she closed her eyes and let the breath escape her lungs in long, happy sighs. "Go down about an inch," she instructed him. "A little to the right. Now up just a smidgen. Ahhh," she murmured as his fingers worked their magic, "that feels delicious."

"Delicious?" Chase chuckled. "How can a back massage feel delicious?" he teased.

"Well, it does, take my word for it. If you're ever

in need of the same treatment, I'll be only too happy to oblige," she promised airily, not embarrassed in the least at the contented sounds she was making.

"I know you have a doctor's appointment in the morning at ten, but are you busy tomorrow evening?" Chase casually asked.

"Mmmm." Jo groaned happily, totally relaxed under the gentle workings of his hands. "I'm not doing anything as far as I can remember. Why?"

"Will you have dinner with me?"

CHAPTER ELEVEN

"Everything is looking just fine, Jo." Marie Edderly smiled as she waved her patient to a chair. "There is one bit of news which I'm certain you'll enjoy hearing though."

"What's that?" Jo asked curiously.

"After examining you today, I'm fairly certain we can look for your baby to be born a little earlier than we'd originally counted on. I thought as much the last time I saw you, but I didn't want to get your hopes up."

"How much earlier?"

"A week, perhaps two. There's nothing for you to worry about," Marie assured her. "But if you have anything you've put off for the last month, I'd go ahead and get it done. You'll probably want to have all your preparations for the baby finished. Babies are notorious for making liars out of us doctors. By the way, there'll be another natural childbirth class starting soon. Are you still interested?"

"Yes," Jo responded eagerly, then took out a pad and wrote down the dates.

On the drive home, Jo found herself nervous, with a tiny spiral of excitement building within her. But she also felt a sense of caution. If the baby did come earlier than planned, then that meant her time with Chase would be shorter as well. Jo found herself torn between the anticipation of her baby and the uncertainty of her relationship with Chase.

Don't worry about it, a tiny voice advised her. He'll still be next door, won't he? Surely after you get your shape back, you'll be capable of rekindling a little of the closeness the two of you have enjoyed. If not, then you'd better figure out a way of being eternally pregnant. Jo pulled a long face at the less than attractive thought, then switched her mind to the evening ahead.

What on earth could she wear that would minimize her bulging tummy and make her look less like a tugboat? In her mind she carefully went over the four dresses in her maternity wardrobe. The most flattering one, and the one that she liked best, was a peach-colored dress. It had tiny puffed sleeves and a moderately round neckline ending in a demur V in the front. The empire waist let the silky material fall in a whispery swirl around her knees.

As soon as she got into the house, she raced to the closet in her bedroom and took out the dress. But how could she expect to look pretty, being as big as she was? Even this dress couldn't hide her protruding stomach. What you need to be concerned about, you ninny, she told herself, is just why your handsome neighbor is asking you out. It certainly can't be the slender, graceful lines of your figure. You look like a circus fat lady.

With a disgusted toss of her dark head, Jo threw the dress back into the closet and slammed the door. She was a fool! She'd been so wrapped up in thoughts of going out with Chase, she hadn't even stopped to consider why he'd asked her. Of course it was pity! He felt sorry for her.

She stalked into the bathroom and turned on the shower, then began jerking off her clothes. By the time she'd showered and was patting herself dry, Jo had decided she didn't want any man's pity—least of all Chase Colbern's. She'd been a fool for allowing him to become such an overwhelming part of her life. It was time she took matters in her own hands, she lectured herself with grim determination. She would start by breaking a dinner date she shouldn't have accepted in the first place.

As Jo dialed the office number Chase had made her write down by both the kitchen and bedroom phones, she found her palms beginning to perspire. When a brisk feminine voice answered, Jo asked for Chase before her courage could desert her. In seconds he was on the line. Jo was certain she'd lost her voice.

"Hello?" Chase repeated, a trace of irritation sounding in the gruff tones.

"Jo here, Chase," she finally managed in what she hoped was a convincing voice. "I—"

"You're late from the doctor's office," he interrupted her. "Is something wrong? Wasn't the doctor happy with your progress? Damn it, Jo, if you aren't telling me everything, I'll wring your neck."

Jo had to grin at his panic, having no difficulty imagining him as he glowered into the phone. "The only thing I haven't told you is that Marie thinks the baby will be a wee bit earlier than we first expected."

"How early?" Chase boomed, the panic becoming more pronounced. "You're not in labor now, are you?"

"By about two weeks, and no, I'm not in labor now. I will have to get going though and finish the nursery. I'm going out this afternoon to look for a bed."

"Scratch that idea," he told her flatly. "I'll take you later this week. Knowing you, you will probably go into labor in some damn department store."

"Er—that's what I called about," she hedged. "This evening. I'm afraid I'm going to have to bow out of having dinner with you."

"Why?" No gentle urging—no subtle pressure.

"I'd forgotten that I promised Mary Clare to work with her on a new idea for next year's Christmas cards."

"I happen to know that Personal Touch Greeting Cards doesn't carry Christmas cards. Try again."

"We're branching out."

"In a pig's eye! Be ready at seven o'clock sharp, Ms. Benoit, or I'll personally dress you myself." The receiver was slammed down, and Jo was left with silence on the other end.

"I take it you and Jo aren't getting along at the moment?" Matthew Colbern peered over his reading glasses at Chase and almost chuckled at the peevish expression on his eldest son's face. He dropped his gaze back down to the contract he was going over. "Your mother and I are really fond of Jo. It isn't easy having a baby alone. I admire her courage."

"I'm delighted you think so highly of her," Chase bit out testily. "I'd also like to know what you meant by that crack?" He'd given his parents a brief sketch of Jo's pregnancy months ago, leaving out the more personal details. He had included that Lance Benoit was the father, however.

"Why—nothing, son," the elder Colbern drawled as he leaned back in his chair, struggling to keep a straight face. "Your mother and I think it's a very admirable thing you're doing, helping Jo at a time like this." To himself, Matthew was thinking he'd never seen a man more royally snafued in his entire life. At the moment Chase reminded him of a wild stallion being slowly and methodically saddle broken.

Chase favored his father with his steely-eyed scrutiny, then turned back to stare out the window. During his conversation with Jo, he'd bounded to his feet when he thought she was in labor, and his body was still trembling from relief at finding that wasn't the case. Something must have upset her to make her want to back out of having dinner with him, he thought moodily as he chewed at the corner of his bottom lip. Or it could be a case of her mule-headedness. In spite of her seemingly easy manner, he'd learned she could be stubborn as hell. Well, he'd take care of that, he promised himself. She was going to dinner with him if he had to tie her to the top of the car.

At precisely six-forty-five, Chase, dressed in a light-tan sports jacket and dark-brown pants, banged a heavy fist against Jo's back door. He really did need a key to her house, he thought irritably. What if she were to go into labor in the middle of the night? There was no way in hell he could get to her without breaking a window. After that time when he'd rescued her from the exercise machine caper, he'd installed safety locks on all the windows. A key was a must.

When there was no answer to his first summons, Chase banged hard enough on the door to break it down. When it was flung open, he found himself facing a very annoyed, short, pregnant Jo, her dark hair still caught up in hot rollers. She was dressed in a loose pink robe that made her look about sixteen.

"Is it necessary to rip the door from its hinges?" she threw at him.

"It wouldn't be if you'd been more prompt." Chase smiled lazily. He whipped his other hand from behind his broad back and settled a dozen long-stemmed yellow roses in her arms.

Jo looked down at the roses, then back at Chase. "Why yellow? Does my being pregnant mean that red ones would have been wasted on me?"

"Not at all," Chase stepped forward and dropped a kiss on her forehead. "It simply means you prefer yellow roses, my little spitfire. You've told me so on more than one occasion. Remember?"

"Oh." Jo sniffed. She turned and hurried into the kitchen, where she rummaged around in a bottom cupboard till she found a vase. "Thank you for the flowers, they're beautiful," she said over her shoulder while filling the vase with water. "You're also early."

Chase walked over close to her and leaned against the counter. "I'm early because I wasn't sure you understood the arrangements," he said close to her ear. He stared at the heavy rollers in her hair and the wire clips holding them in place. "Don't those things hurt?"

"What?" she asked, her fingers busy arranging the roses.

158

"These," he said softly. Without asking permission, he began removing the rollers from her hair.

"Don't do that," Jo said crossly, slapping at his hands. "My hair will be straight as a board."

"Nonsense." Chase frowned. "Only last week you were complaining about it being too curly. Besides, I like your hair just as it is. It reminds me of a splash of velvet."

"It does?" Jo murmured nervously, then forced herself to look up at him. What she saw wasn't the old frowning, gruff Chase. Instead she found a man with a teasing light in his eyes, eyes that were looking at her as if she were the tastiest morsel on an hors d'oeuvre tray. "It's—it's nothing like that at all," she stammered. "If you'll excuse me," she said hurriedly, "I'll go finish dressing." The entire time she was speaking, she was edging toward the hall door. One hand was clamped against the remaining curlers in her hair, while the other hand grabbed at the top button of her robe, which had fallen open. "Er—make yourself at home," she suggested, then flew down the hall to her bedroom.

Jo sped across the room toward the closet, leaving a trail of hot rollers behind her. What on earth was the matter with Chase? she kept asking herself as she struggled into the peach-color dress. He was acting like . . . like . . . No, no, she cautioned her overactive imagination, don't even think it. He's merely in a teasing mood. He knows he was short with you on the phone earlier today and this is his way of making amends. Of course it is.

But somewhere in the back of her mind, the thought still persisted that there *was* something different about Chase. For a moment there in the kitchen, she'd thought he was about to take her in his arms and kiss her. The thought, while rather pleasant, scared Jo to death. She knew for a fact that Chase Colbern wasn't an amateur when it came to seducing women. At that moment Jo caught a glimpse of her generous shape in the mirror of the dresser. A grimace pulled at her lips. "Don't be ridiculous," she muttered. "Seduction in your particular case would be something for the *Guinness Book of World Records!"*

She had just jerked the dress into place and was attempting to reach the elusive zipper when the door to the bedroom opened and Chase strolled in.

Jo gaped at him as if a ghostly apparition had suddenly sprung into her midst. "This is my bedroom," she informed him feebly.

"And quite a nice room it is." Chase smiled that lazy grin she was still unaccustomed to. He walked over to her, his sharp gaze taking in the peculiar twisted position of her body as she groped at her backside. "Having trouble?" he asked unperturbed. Without the slightest hesitation, he stepped behind her, found the zipper, then slid it into place. "That better?" The touch of his warm fingers lingering on her neck were doing the strangest things to her breathing.

"Fine," Jo said hurriedly. She moved over to the dresser and began brushing her hair, thankful that she'd already put on her makeup. Her hands were trembling so badly that she doubted she could even have grasped the shadow applicator.

"I forgot to give you this." Chase further confounded her by walking up behind her. He slipped both arms around her and placed a small package tied with a gold ribbon on the dresser in front of her. Instead of moving, he remained where he was, and the entire length of Jo's body was smack against his.

She took a deep breath, her head dizzy from the unexpectedness of this totally different Chase. Tentatively she picked up the package and removed the paper, careful not to move any part of her body but her arms and hands. The steady thumping of Chase's heart against her back and the embarrassing racing of her own were causing enough problems.

Once the paper was removed, Jo saw a small, beautifully designed crystal container of Giorgio perfume. Without thinking, she smiled. She raised her head and met the bold gaze sharing the mirror with her. "A favorite of yours?" she asked pointedly.

"No, you minx." Chase chuckled. He turned her in his arms, his hands locking behind, at her waist.

"I can't recall giving any woman perfume in years. You mentioned it last night, so I assumed you liked it."

"Oh, I do," Jo admitted reluctantly, "I do. What sane woman wouldn't?" She opened the bottle and touched the tip of the cap to her throat and wrists. "Mmmm." She briefly closed her eyes and inhaled the delicate scent. "It smells delicious."

"Of course, what else?" Chase smiled. "Are you ready?"

"I suppose so." Jo sighed. "There really isn't much else I can do to myself, is there?"

"There's nothing else that needs doing," she was told in a husky voice. "There is, however, one thing you can do for me."

"What?"

"Kiss me."

"Kiss you?"

"Am I so distasteful to you?"

"Oh, no. It's just—I mean . . ."

"Do you find me repulsive?"

"Uh-uh."

"Then what's the problem?"

"I'm pregnant."

"I kind of figured as much. And if you get much larger, I'll have to buy some arm extenders." A sharp kick on his shins was his reward for such a remark. "Bad tempered though you are, shrew that you are, I still want that kiss."

"Don't play with me."

"Lady, I assure you, I've never been more serious in my entire life."

"Since when?"

"Since you hit me in the behind with that damned scooter."

"Well . . . since you put it that way—"

Jo clutched the perfume in one hand, then reached up with the other and brought his head down to hers. Her lips touched his hesitantly at first, but Chase had other ideas. He took command of the situation, and in seconds Jo knew the warmth that was spreading throughout her entire body wasn't some sudden attack of high blood pressure. His lips coaxed and teased her mouth into willing submission, leaving her shamelessly welcoming his tongue into an erotic exchange with her own that had her senses cresting on a tidal wave of desire.

It was Chase who eased back, his stunned blue eyes dark and glowing as he stared down into her face. "Pregnant or not, Ms. Benoit," he whispered hoarsely, "you are one hell of a sexy lady."

CHAPTER TWELVE

A few weeks later Jo was lying in bed, staring at the ceiling above her. The nap she was supposed to be taking had turned into a time for her vivid imagination to run wild. The closer her due date, the more nervous she became. Funny, but having a baby had always been an event she had looked forward to—under normal circumstances. Unfortunately, there was nothing normal about her situation. How would she be able to juggle her time between the demands of her job and the caring of an infant? Could she handle it?

Of course you can, she told herself. You aren't the first woman to have a baby alone, and you certainly won't be the last. So why are you feeling sorry for yourself? You have a career you enjoy, you own your own home, and, for what it's worth, you have a family. The only thing that's lacking in your life is a husband. Considering Lance and his own problems, don't you think you're better off? Besides, what could a husband do that hasn't already been taken care of by Chase?

Chase. Jo turned onto her side as the picture of Chase drifted through her thoughts. She hadn't asked for his help, but he'd given it just the same. As she looked back on the peculiar pattern their lives had taken, she couldn't pinpoint the exact moment she had come to depend on him. That she had become dependent on him at all bothered her. All her adult life Jo had taken pride in running her life. She'd battled her family and won, she'd refused to allow Lance to keep her shackled to a life she found unacceptable. So why had she given in so easily when Chase appeared on the scene?

That first week or so after learning she was pregnant was understandable. Her world had been absolute chaos. But as she began to accept the inevitable, why hadn't she recaptured that same fighting instinct she'd been born with and told Chase to stop managing her life?

Because you care for him. The timing couldn't be worse, but if you're the realist you say you are, then you have to accept that Chase Colbern means more to you than an overly concerned neighbor. And now, even her social life, what there was of it, had been taken over by Chase.

Having dinner with him that first time had set the course for most of her evenings during the next few weeks, a fact that Jo found difficult to deal with. It wasn't that she didn't enjoy being with Chase, it was simply the uncertainty of the outcome that plagued her thoughts.

The evening before, for example, she and Chase had had dinner at his parents' home. It was the second time in as many weeks, and Jo was terrified his family would begin to think she was using Chase.

She'd tried to explain her feelings to him when they'd returned to her house, but no amount of arguing could convince him.

"My folks adore you," he'd told her. "Even if they didn't, I'm way past the age when I need or want parental approval of whom I see."

"But, Chase—" Jo had squirmed around on the sofa till she was facing his sprawled figure, his feet propped on the edge of the coffee table. "You must admit our situation is slightly different from most relationships between two unmarried people."

"In what way?" he'd infuriated her by asking, throwing one arm up to ward off the throw pillow she sailed at him in exasperation. "Come on." He had tried to ease her out of her dark mood. "I don't think you're a scheming hussy, and neither do my folks. In fact," he'd added, frowning at her from beneath heavy brows, "I was almost tempted to tell my dad and my baby brother to keep their damn paws off you this evening."

"Chase!" Jo's eyes had grown round as saucers. "How can you even think such evil things about your father?"

"Because I have a sick mind." He'd leered at her, laughing at her profound shock. "If I promise not to think of my father as a lecherous old man, can I still have a swing at Simon? He's always been an irritating kid."

"I give up." Jo'd sighed defeatedly. She crossed her arms over her breasts and stared straight ahead. "You're incorrigible. You're also small-minded and harbor evil thoughts about your family." Chase had laughed at her silly notions, but Jo worried nonetheless.

Mary Clare considered Jo to be paranoid on the subject of Chase and his attention.

"Why are you worried?" The attractive blonde had looked at Jo as they talked over a cup of coffee in Jo's kitchen. "No one is putting a gun to Chase's head, sweetie. Personally I find it touching. You've managed to stumble upon a man who seems to care for you without all the usual razzmatazz we gals have to go through."

"But I'm pregnant, for heaven's sake!" Jo exclaimed. "Our social life is hardly the liveliest on record, and I just happen to look like a whale. Doesn't it strike you as odd that a man in Chase's position would choose to spend most of his free time with a woman in my condition? He's single, wealthy, and I don't have to tell you how sexy he is. It doesn't add up."

Mary Clare leaned forward and murmured in a confidential tone, "Do you think he's some sort of weirdo who gets turned on by short, pregnant brunettes?" When her words were met with frigid silence, she tried again. "You didn't look like a whale when you first met Chase. Have you thought of that?"

But Jo wasn't convinced.

The abrupt ringing of the phone jolted her from her disturbing thoughts. She reached across the bed and lifted the receiver to her ear. "Hello?"

"Hi, Jo. This is Jake. I hate to do this to you, but I've come down with a terrible cold. I'm afraid I won't be able to go with you to your Lamaze class tonight."

"Don't worry about the class, Jake, just take care of yourself," Jo assured him, her heart sinking as she replaced the receiver.

She had attended the previous classes alone, learning how tense muscles could cause unnecessary pain and discomfort and how, by learning to relax those same muscles, a woman could alleviate a great deal of her pain. She learned the suggested exercises and practiced them faithfully. But tonight she was to begin the breathing exercises, and Jo had wanted Jake with her.

She rolled to the side of the bed and sat on the edge, going over in her mind the probable list of candidates at her disposal. Her father and brothers were out of the question. Frank Kincaid was too busy, his own medical practice occupying every minute of his spare time. Jo could well imagine her brothers' outcry if she were to suggest either of them accompany her. And her mother was far too busy. Mo? She grinned in spite of herself as she visualized him in a room filled with pregnant women. No, Mo was a dear, but she had a pretty good idea he would panic. That left Chase. No, it didn't, Jo told herself. She'd allowed him to force her to eat food that she didn't want to eat, take her on long hikes she hated, dictate her bedtime and an endless list of other unpleasant duties. She wasn't about to allow Chase to be her partner in class. He would become a complete dictator in her life.

As Chase drove into his garage, he glanced next door, noting the red VW was parked in the driveway. He got out of the car, reached for the briefcase that had become his constant companion of late, then went into the house.

A bout of sneezing could be heard the minute he entered the kitchen. Chase looked at Jake's watery eyes and red nose, then frowned. "You should be in bed."

"It's just a cold." The older man shrugged.

"Colds turn into flu. Half the office staff is out sick," Chase told him. "Have you had a doctor check you over?"

"No," Jake barked, "and I don't intend to, either. I have my own remedies for curing the common cold. Dinner will be ready in about thirty minutes."

"Aren't we eating kind of early? Do you have plans for this evening?"

"I've cancelled my plans," Jake snapped.

"Oh? What were they?" Chase asked.

"If you must know, I was going to class with Jo."

"Was she able to get someone else?"

"I doubt it. You don't just pick someone off the street and take them to natural childbirth classes," Jake retorted, glowering at him.

Chase mulled over this bit of sharply delivered truth, feeling more than a little peeved that Jo hadn't called him. In fact, he had been annoyed from the start that she'd asked Jake instead of him. "Well," Chase said with a shrug, "I'm sure she'll work it out."

"Now that's a fine how d' you do!" Jake threw up his hands and turned back to the counter. "That poor little thing needs help, and all you can say is 'I'm sure she'll work it out.' "

"What the hell do you want me to do?" Chase demanded. "Lie down in front of her car and beg her to let me accompany her?"

"That would be mighty neighborly of you," Jake threw over his shoulder in an icy voice.

"That's a crock of bull, and you know it. She obviously doesn't want me with her or she would have asked me."

"Since when have you waited to be asked?" Jake swung around and pinned Chase with an accusing stare. "From the beginning you've just about run Jo's life from sunup to sundown. I didn't notice you waiting to be asked when the nursery needed painting or the wallpaper needed hanging or the closet needed remodeling. Did she ask you to go out and find her a car? Did she ask you to keep an eye on her all these months like a broody hen with one chick?"

"All right!" Chase sighed angrily. "I get the message. I'll make myself available when she's ready to go. If she wants me to go along, I will. Does that make you happy, you psalm-singing old busybody?"

"It helps." Jake sniffed frostily. Privately, he was jumping with glee. From the first moment Jo had asked him to attend the classes with her, Jake had known that somehow, by hook or crook, he was going to get Chase to exchange places with him. He never thought he'd see the day when a cold would be looked upon as a gift from heaven, but it was, and he was delighted—simply delighted.

Dinner was a quiet occasion, to say the least. Bink was spending the night with a friend, leaving Jake and Chase to stare crossly at each other across the table.

"How's work?" Jake finally broke the silence.

"Boring as hell." Chase made no effort to carry the conversation.

"If you would put as much time and effort into

171

looking for good things about it instead of only seeing the bad, you might find you enjoy the change."

"When I want a pep talk, Jake, I'll let you know. What time is this shindig supposed to start?"

"You mean Jo's classes?"

"Hell, yes, 'Jo's classes.'"

"Seven o'clock. You'd better get a move on. It's six-twenty. She might decide to leave early."

"I should be so lucky," Chase muttered. He downed the last of his iced tea, then pushed back his chair and stood. "I'll be ready in five minutes, but in case you hear her car start up"—he smiled grimly—"why don't you run over and flag her down?"

Ten minutes later Chase was leaning against the fender of the VW in Jo's driveway. He was about to give up his post and go on in, when the door opened and Jo stepped out.

She looked startled when she saw him. Not from his actual presence, but from the fact that he'd never before hesitated to bang on her door if he wanted to see her, or even barge in if she didn't answer quickly enough.

"Is something wrong?"

"Nothing that I know of," Chase replied levelly, his chilly tone not lost on Jo.

She searched for some plausible explanation for his behavior, but found nothing. "I'm afraid I have

172

to be going then." She smiled faintly. "My class starts at seven, and the traffic is usually heavy at this time of day."

"I'm well aware of your plans for the evening, Ms. Benoit," Chase informed her. "What I'm having trouble accepting, however, is why you didn't call me when Jake told you he couldn't go."

"The reason I didn't ask you, Chase, is simple. I don't want you going with me."

"You didn't want me?" he repeated, stunned.

"You heard me." Jo lifted her stubborn chin a fraction of an inch. "I realize now that it's as much my fault as yours, but do you realize that you have completely taken over my life?"

"Only when I think you're in danger of hurting yourself or the baby." Chase thrust his own granite chin forward. "There's no rhyme or reason in your life. Order is something you've dismissed from your vocabulary. You remind me of a one-legged man at a dance, hopping around with no sense of direction at all."

"Are you finished?" Jo asked haughtily.

"Hell, no!" Chase reached out and grabbed her arm. "You might not want me, but I'll be damned if you're going to that class tonight by yourself. I should have been the one you asked in the first place. Jake is an old man. What does he know about having babies?"

"Jealousy!" Jo murmured amazed as she was hustled across the yard to Chase's car.

"What's that supposed to mean?" He gave her a suspicious look as he put her in the car and slammed the door.

Jo waited until he was behind the wheel. "I never dreamed you were jealous when I asked Jake to work with me. Why didn't you say something before now?"

"Because I thought eventually it might occur to you to consider my feelings." He started the engine, then roared down the driveway and into the street.

Jo was more perplexed than before. For the life of her, she couldn't understand this latest outburst. Chase was acting for all the world as if this baby were his and that she had tried to deprive him of some important event. She shook her head. Men were the strangest creatures.

"If I've hurt your feelings, Chase, then I apologize. I feel guilty considering what you've already done for me. And," she forced herself to go on bravely, "it looks to me as if we've gotten ourselves involved in something neither of us understand. At least—I don't."

"You sure as hell don't, lady" was his terse comment.

"That's another thing," Jo continued stubbornly. "You treat me like a child. I resent that. I may very well remind you of a one-legged man at a dance, but it's my dance. I'll have my baby, and I'll take care of it."

"Just like that, huh?" Chase threw her a cold look. "And afterward? What then?"

"Why—I suppose I'll go on with my life as usual. At least, as much as one can with a newborn. It's done every day, you know. You'd be surprised at the number of single mothers there are. It might shock you to know that almost half of the members of this class we're going to are single. I haven't pried into the reasons why, but I certainly don't feel out of place."

"A child needs a father," he intoned piously.

"So it does," Jo agreed, hiding a smile. "Perhaps someday my child will have a father. I'll certainly give the thought every consideration. Does that make you happy?"

Chase took his eyes off the traffic long enough to stare disbelievingly at her. Christ! She looked normal enough, she even acted normal most of the time. But . . . she was, without a doubt, the flakiest dame he'd ever run into in his entire life—except maybe for his mother. He turned his attention back to his driving, his mind whirling like a spinning top. How was it possible that with all the women he knew he had fallen in love with this warm, vibrant, talented, and absolutely nutty slip of a beauty sitting beside him?

CHAPTER THIRTEEN

"Well?" Jo grinned. "What do you think so far?" She was lying on a thin pad on the floor, a pillow beneath her knees.

Chase, sitting cross-legged beside her, looked around. As far as the eye could see, there was nothing but huge tummies from which legs were extended. The only woman not pregnant was the instructor and Marie Edderly, Jo's doctor. Most of the other men present had been to several classes, and Chase, much to Jo's delight, wasn't the least embarrassed.

"I think," Chase whispered with a chuckle as he leaned over her, "this is the fattest group of ladies I've ever seen."

"You fink!" she hissed. "You have no respect for motherhood."

Chase was denied his comeback as the instructor called the class to order after the short break. The next phase to be discussed was breathing. Jo had done her homework well and was eager to try it out.

She kept one eye on the instructor, the other on Chase, who was—along with the other men—attempting to follow directions.

Suddenly Jo giggled, bringing a frosty glare from Chase.

"May I ask what you find so funny?" he whispered, while he attempted the final stage of short shallow breaths recommended during the apex of a contraction.

"You're what's funny," she whispered back. "You look like a huge blowfish."

Chase had to laugh despite himself, which promptly ended an otherwise fine performance. Fortunately that was the end of the breathing exercise, as well as the class for the evening. He slumped against the wall. "Damn!" he exclaimed in an undertone. "Having a baby is tiring. Are you sure you're up to all this?"

"Oh, my!" Jo batted her lashes demurely. "Do you mean I actually have a choice in the matter at this stage of the game?"

Chase smiled wryly and rubbed his chin. "No, I don't suppose you do." He pushed himself to his feet, then reached down and caught Jo under the arms and hauled her to her feet. "Many more sessions of this, woman, and my poor back will be broken."

"There must be some reason why I don't feel the slightest bit of pity for you," she said lightly. She reached down and picked up the pillow. Chase retrieved the pad.

"I see you brought someone with you," Marie Edderly remarked as she walked up.

"Kidnapped is more like it," Jo laughingly replied in hopes of keeping Chase from feeling hemmed in. "Marie, this is Chase Colbern, a neighbor. This lovely lady, as I pointed out to you earlier, Chase, is my doctor."

After telling Chase that she'd known Jo since she was a youngster, Marie thanked him for coming. "Having a partner share the class is very helpful to the expectant mother. I don't know if Jo has told you, but we have a number of single mothers these days. I'm always so pleased when I see a man coming in with them."

"If your patient hadn't been so close-mouthed, I would have been with her when the classes began," Chase said easily, enjoying the rosy flush that crept over Jo's cheeks. "She's very independent, you know."

"I do indeed." Marie laughed, her green eyes running appreciatively over Jo's rugged escort. "If she thinks she can do without you, please feel free to come alone. I'm sure we have others in the class who would enjoy having you with them."

"Mind your own business, Marie," Jo interrupted their teasing. "I'm sure your little mothers are quite capable of finding their own men."

"Oh, well." Marie smiled. "I was only trying to

do my civic duty." She patted Jo on the shoulder. "Remember, you have another appointment on Monday. Bye, Chase." She flashed him a warm smile and walked away.

"Busybody," Jo muttered as they left the building.

"I liked her," Chase murmured smoothly. He was more than a little pleased by the way Jo had declared him off limits to the other women. He dropped a long arm around Jo's shoulders and pulled her close to him. "Is she a family friend?"

"Something like that."

"Is she married? She's a very attractive woman."

"Really?" Jo snapped. "Would you like me to see if I can get you a date with her?" She glared up at him. Attractive indeed! she fumed. She jerked away from Chase and waddled the remaining distance to the car alone. What added fuel to her anger were Marie Edderly's age and career. She was in her middle thirties, and Jo knew Chase would be forty on his next birthday. America's ideal couple, she thought savagely as she sat waiting for Chase to walk around the car and get in.

Chase inserted the key into the ignition but made no effort to start the engine. He turned toward Jo, his brows arching knowingly as he took in the tense line of her lips and the rigid set of her shoulders. He was tempted to laugh at the comical picture she made, but thought better of that idea.

He was learning, during these last weeks of his "beloved's" pregnancy, that when crossed, she had quite a temper.

"Hungry?" he asked the magic word of late.

"A little," he was told in a stilted tone.

"Chinese, hamburgers, or sauerkraut?" He could almost see the tiny wheels of her mind as they waged their individual war of preference. "We could get all three, if the decision is that difficult to make." He smiled.

Jo looked at him then, and her heart stood still. She saw a rugged, tanned face that could be gentle, warm, and as unyielding as granite. She saw the straight edges of his strong white teeth between the parted lines of his lips. His startlingly blue eyes never failed to remind her of that special blue intermingled with the orange burst of color just before sundown. His hair lay flat against his head and still bore the sunstreaks from the summer. This was a man she'd come to know—in some ways—more intimately than she'd known her husband. This was a man whose face, whose touch, even the sound of his voice, would be a part of her for as long as she lived.

"Jo?" Chase looked concerned. He reached out and placed a palm against the angle of her cheek. "Are you all right, sweetheart?"

She gave herself a mental shake, then smiled. "I'm fine. Why don't we have hamburgers, tons of fries, and a milkshake?"

"You'll have hamburgers, fries, and a milk-shake." Chase basked in her smile. "I'll have black coffee and watch you eat."

True to his word, Chase didn't eat a single thing, but Jo wasn't in the least daunted by his abstinence. By the time Chase got her home, she was so sleepy, she could barely keep her eyes open.

"I'm sorry for being such a party pooper." She opened her eyes when she felt the car come to a halt. "But I'm positive they put a sleeping pill in my shake."

"Think nothing of it." Chase laughed as he hoisted her out of the car and guided her inside. "Not too long ago you were complaining of not being able to rest. Now you can't seem to get enough. You're a very wish-washy lady, Ms. Benoit."

"The privileges of my sex, Mr. Colbern." She nodded sleepily against his chest.

At the door, Chase took out the key he'd had Jo give him and unlocked the door. "Can you make it all right on your own?"

"Maybe," she teased him. "If I have any trouble brushing my teeth or getting into my gown, I'll be sure to yell. Okay?"

"If you want me to sta—" Chase began, then stopped, an expression of such tenderness welling in his gaze that Jo felt her pulse quicken. "If you need me during the night, sing out." He leaned

181

down and kissed her briefly but hard on the lips, then turned and walked away.

Jo closed the door, a pensive expression on her face. She wondered what it was Chase had started to say. But drowsiness and the need for sleep far outweighed her ability to reason. I'm sure it was nothing, she told herself, staggering down the hall to her bedroom.

"But what on earth is it, and how does it work?" Jo looked at the contraption on her bedside table with misgivings. "I'm not very good with any sort of electrical equipment, you know."

"Nonsense." Chase grunted. Only his lower half was visible to the unconvinced Jo, for his head was under her bed. "A four-year-old can operate this system. Hand me that adjustable wrench, honey."

Jo looked down at the large triple-drawered tool box, not having the faintest idea what an adjustable wrench was. She did notice one particular tool lying to one side. "Does it look like a pac-man with a tail?" she asked earnestly.

"Mmmm—" Chase hesitated for a few seconds, not knowing whether to laugh out loud or keep his amusement to himself. Considering that his rear was an excellent target for any revenge Jo might have in mind, he opted for the latter. "I've never thought about it quite like that, but I suppose it does. Er—would you hand me the pac-man wrench, please?"

After another few minutes of grunts, peculiar sounds, and a few well-chosen curse words, Chase eased his way out from beneath the bed. He remained seated on the floor, busily twisting and connecting a black cord to the box on the table.

"I really think this a lot of unnecessary trouble for you," Jo told him from her perch on the side of the bed. She was dressed in a pair of jeans and a pink top. In place of shoes, her feet were snug in a pair of white ribbed socks. Swollen ankles, she'd decided, were one of the more distasteful things about being pregnant.

"What if you were to go into labor in the middle of the night?" Chase asked her.

"I'd call you, of course."

"Ahhh"—he smiled sweetly—"but what if my line was busy? Or what if the receiver had been accidentally left off the hook? What then?"

"Why, I suppose I would walk over and ring the doorbell." Really, she thought with a frown, Chase had the most irritating way of turning the simplest thing into an emergency.

"You probably would." He shook his head in defeat. "And that poor little baby would wind up being born somewhere between our respective back doors." He tapped the black box decisively. "Use this instead. All you have to do is flip this switch, press this button, and wait for me to answer. Using an intercom is much more convenient than having a pregnant woman stumble around in the dark."

"I'll use it." Jo glared at him. "Are you sure you don't have the toilet seat wired as well?"

"Tsk, tsk," Chase needled her. "Are you sure you feel up to going shopping? You're awfully grouchy today."

"I'm going," Jo said determinedly. "I refuse to let my baby be born without having a bed. I can't bear for him to arrive in this world and not feel wanted."

"I seriously doubt the lack of a baby bed would cause an infant to suffer emotionally," Chase hooted as he got to his feet. "And where do you get off calling it a 'he'? What if it's a girl?"

"He, she. I'm not hard to please. Although I do have a lovely boy's name all picked out."

"A boy's name is not lovely." Chase snorted. "What is it?"

"Ian Michael."

"Nice. I like it. But what if it's a girl?"

"My mind's a total blank."

"Now *that's* something to cause a kid emotional stress," Chase quipped, "the fact that her own mother couldn't even come up with a name for her."

"I didn't say I couldn't," Jo bristled. "It's—it's —been difficult."

"Name her after her mother," Chase suggested, then frowned. "What the devil *is* your real name?"

"I'd rather die than tell."

"Okay." He shrugged. "But I bet that bluenosed sister of yours would be delighted to tell me."

"Josephine Evangeline," Jo informed him, the angry glint in her gray eyes defying him to show the tiniest flicker of amusement.

"Judas Priest!" Chase exclaimed. "Who the hell dumped something like that on a poor, defenseless baby?"

"My grandmother."

"No wonder you want to keep it quiet. If I were you, I'd sue my parents." Jo promptly burst into a fit of silly giggles.

"Can you imagine"—she gasped when she could speak again—"what my family's reaction would be if I were to actually do such a thing?"

That malicious train of thought kept Jo amused all the way from her house to the department store where she'd seen the crib she wanted.

"It's right over here," she told Chase, her hand gripping his arm as she urged him along. "If that wimp sold it, I'll murder him," she muttered when she didn't see the crib. "It was gorgeous, simply gorgeous. The wood was mahogany, and it had the most beautiful carving at both ends and along the sides."

"May I help you?" a gushy, condescending voice broke into their midst. Jo and Chase turned and looked at the bald, portly gentleman, dressed in a horrible red and purple checked sports jacket and matching red pants. For a moment both their mouths dropped open at the apparition before them. Chase was the first to recover.

"We're interested in a crib."

"I should certainly hope so," the twit had the nerve to retort, his myopic gaze surveying Jo's hefty figure with something akin to disbelief. "When is the little lady expecting?"

"Well, she—" Chase began.

"The 'little lady' didn't come in here to give you an update on her pregnancy," Jo interrupted, taking a menacing step toward the object of her anger. "You had a mahogany crib right here"—she pointed to the spot where she was standing—"two days ago. Have you sold it?"

"We-lll," the silly man twittered. "Aren't we in a bad mood this evening." He started to say something else, but when Chase stepped forward and the salesman got a good look at the size and breadth of the little lady's "husband," his jaws clamped together like a steel trap. "The crib's been moved over to our finer furniture section," he informed them coolly, indicating, with a nod of his shiny pate, the section farther toward the front of the store. "I'm sure you'll be able to find someone there to help you. Good evening," he announced loftily. He spun around on his black patent heel and strolled off.

"Twerp!" Jo hissed.

"The 'little lady' mustn't get so upset," Chase leaned close to her ear and whispered. "Why don't

186

we see if we can find your crib?" he further suggested, his voice quivering with suppressed laughter.

"You think it's funny, don't you?" Jo demanded as they made their way past an impressive display of expensive sofas and chairs.

"Indeed I do not," Chase informed her solemnly, keeping a steady hand beneath her elbow. "I was ready to defend you, my little spitfire, the moment you got through scratching that poor man's eyes out."

She cast a skeptical glance toward him. "Was I that bad?"

"Certainly not," Chase lied with a straight face.

"There it is!" Jo exclaimed the moment they passed the last sofa and turned the corner. She rushed over to where several pieces of baby furniture were on display, running her hands lovingly over a crib that even Chase had to admit was the work of a superb craftsman.

"It's very nice." He nodded, after poking and inspecting each groove and screw.

"Nice? It's beautiful. All my children will sleep in this crib."

"I'm sure each of them will be gratified by their mother's good taste," he said dryly. "But will you please do one small favor for me?"

"What's that?" Jo asked absently, her attention still held by the exquisite detail given to the crib.

187

"Will you please consult with me before you begin your next child? Seeing you through a pregnancy has been the most unnerving experience of my entire life."

CHAPTER FOURTEEN

"Get me any information you can find on the last big job Overton has bid on, Laura," Chase told the secretary as he strode through her office. "You may have to call on one or two of your spies I know you've got tucked away over there. Oh and by the way, see if my dad has a few free minutes. I can go to him, or he can come to my office."

"Will do." Laura Channing favored Chase's retreating back with a pleased grin. From the sound of his voice, it looked as if he'd finally settled in. Not daunted in the least by his reference to her unique way of learning the enemy's secrets, she opened a desk drawer and took out her little black book. She pursed her mouth thoughtfully as she opened the book to a certain page.

Once in his office, Chase removed his jacket, rolled back the sleeves of his white shirt, and loosened his tie. He rubbed his palms together in an unconscious gesture of anticipation of the information Laura would have on his desk in due time. For the first time since his return to Houston, he'd found something he was eager to get to work on.

Chase had gotten a call earlier in the day from Jim Abbott. They'd been friends since college, and, since both were engineers, they'd run into each other in some very exotic spots around the world. Chase was quite surprised to learn that Jim had recently been fired from a rival firm. They'd made plans to meet for lunch, and Chase found himself looking forward not only to seeing his old friend, but of having a chance to talk shop with someone who'd lived the same life as he.

After a series of "remember whens" and several good-natured put-downs regarding past exploits, Jim mentioned a contract his former firm was getting ready to bid on and said frankly that he didn't see how they could do the job. Not only had they fired him, but they'd let two other engineers go as well. A nephew of the owner had taken control. His first move had been to replace reliable, experienced personnel with younger, more "progressive" minds.

"Did you try to talk with him?" Chase asked.

"Hell, yes." Jim frowned. "I've been with the Overton outfit for fifteen years. I'd never paid much attention to the rumors floating around about the nephew, but when he suddenly made a power play and gained control, we were all caught up short. The day I finally got in to see him, you'd have thought I was a stranger. He barely gave me ten minutes."

"This contract you mentioned. Sounds like a

pretty big job. I don't recall hearing anything about it."

"Ahhh." Jim chuckled. "Most likely you won't either. Rumor is, the nephew has friends in Washington. Seems like the only companies to know that bids were ready to be received were a few small firms and, of course, Overton's. At the time, I wondered how you guys over at Colbern had let such a plum slip by."

"It's difficult to bid on a contract when you aren't aware one is available," Chase replied with a grin.

Their food came, and Jim's lingering gaze followed the shapely waitress as she left their table. "Your mouth is open," Chase taunted him as he dug into the thick, sizzling steak.

"Mmmm." Jim shook his head. "Women. Wonderful creatures."

"I take it you're still a bachelor?"

Jim stared at him as if he'd lost his mind. "Listen." He wagged his fork at Chase. "It took me damned near three years to get my ex-wife married off. I was beginning to think I'd have to pay her alimony for the rest of my natural life."

"You married her off?" Chase asked incredulously.

"I even paid for one of those dating services for her. I was desperate, I tell you. She finally picked off a wealthy rancher from Wyoming. Seemed like a nice fellow too. Last time I saw him, though, he looked grim, mean. We had a few drinks together, and for a moment I thought he was going to offer her back to me. I patted him on the shoulder and got the hell out of there."

"Wise decision." Chase laughed. "Seriously, though, Jim, don't you ever get the urge to settle down?" It was odd. Being with Jim brought back pleasant memories, but it also thrust into clear focus the emptiness of Chase's own life before meeting Jo. Oh, he had family, especially Bink, but there was a vast difference in loving one's child and being "in love" with another person. Yet he questioned whether that kind of love was strong enough to satisfy him. Would he be content to stay with her when the urge to seek new frontiers hit him?

"So that's about it." Jim Abbott's voice broke through the conflicting emotions at war within Chase's mind. "I guess what I'm trying to say, Chase, is that I'm an engineer. Frankly, I haven't seen anything or anyone who made me want to change."

"Have you talked with any of the other firms in Houston about a job?"

"Taggert's made me an offer, and so has Frey's. But they're not into the big jobs, Chase. I like working abroad. Most of their work is in the States. Although Frey's has submitted a bid on a couple of oversea contracts."

Suddenly an idea occurred to Chase. "How about coming to work for Colbern?"

Jim leaned back in his chair, his own expression as thoughtful as Chase's. "A job isn't what I had in mind when I called and asked you to have lunch with me. You know the salary an engineer with my kind of experience makes, and I've invested wisely."

"I'm well aware of why you called, Jim, and believe me, I was delighted to hear from you," Chase admitted. "Being chained to a desk after years of being outdoors made your call seem like a ray of sunshine. Seriously, though, my dad is going to retire in a few months, and—whether I like it or not—I'm afraid it falls on me to try and take his place."

"That's great." Jim nodded. "You'll do a good job."

Chase shrugged. "That remains to be seen. With me in the office, though, it does leave a vacancy. You know the types of jobs we go after and the way we treat our employees. Think about it. If you feel you could be happy with us, give me a ring in a couple of days. In the meantime, I think I'll do some checking on that Overton job." He grinned. "I have a friend or two in Washington as well."

By the time the two men parted, Chase had the name of the project currently seeking bids and Jim Abbott knew in his own mind that in two days' time he would be working for Colbern Engineers.

Laura entered Chase's office just ahead of Matthew Colbern. "I wasn't able to find out much, Chase," she told him, placing the single sheet of paper on his desk. "My sources tell me that the project is a hydroelectric dam." She named a Third World country where the dam was to be built. "I did learn, however, the approximate figures of the Overton bid."

"Has anyone ever told you that you're fantastic, Laura?" Chase smiled broadly. He rose to his feet, caught the startled secretary's face between his hands, and kissed her. "I won't forget this," he promised.

"If I were ten years younger, you can be sure I wouldn't let you," the crimson-faced Laura replied.

"Why, Laura," Matthew Colbern said from the opened doorway of the office, "you've worked for me for years, and you've never blushed so nicely when I've complimented you."

"There are compliments and then there are compliments, boss," she remarked pertly as she swept past him, her feet barely touching the floor.

Matthew looked over his shoulder for a second, then turned his head back around to Chase. "Don't you think she's a little old for you, son?" There was a decided twinkle in the elder Colbern's eyes, and a pleased expression as well.

"It's always been my philosophy to keep the women in my life happy. If I can pull this off, I'll kiss Laura three times a day for the rest of her life," Chase muttered, his eyes quickly going over the information he'd requested.

"What's that?" Matthew asked. He walked over and stood beside his son, curious to see what had gotten Chase so excited. Whatever it was, Matthew was thinking, he was grateful. Keeping Chase in Houston was of paramount importance to the firm. His other two sons were hard workers, and he was proud of them. Simon headed up the accounting office, and Brent was in charge of purchasing. But neither of them, if put in control, could keep Colbern Engineering afloat for more than six months. Chase, on the other hand, was a natural.

"This, Dad, is information on a job Overton's is bidding on. They think they've got this contract sewn up, but I think I can stop them."

Matthew looked closer, surprise registering in his face. "This is news to me. How did you happen to hear of it?"

Chase sat back and looked up at his dad. "I had lunch today with Jim Abbott. Remember him?" At Matthew's confirming nod, he went on. "He was fired from Overton's a couple of weeks ago. During our conversation, he mentioned this particular job. Normally a project this size is fairly well circulated among the larger engineering firms, especially firms who've done business with the government in the past."

195

"And?" Matthew prodded as he sat down, excitement showing in his face.

"Jim told me all he knew, as well as voicing his opinion that Overton's wasn't capable of getting the job done. When I got back here, I put Laura on it, and this is what she came up with. By the way, I offered Jim a job. I know how he works, and I believe he'll be an asset to the company. Do you have any problems with that decision?"

"None at all," Matthew agreed. "In fact, hiring Abbott takes a load off my mind."

"In what way?"

"You. I was hoping you'd stay here in Houston," Matthew confessed, "but I wasn't one hundred percent sure you would."

Chase dropped back in his chair, rubbing at his chin with a forefinger. "I'll admit it's been an adjustment. On the other hand, I don't have much of a choice, do I?"

"Of course you have a choice."

"Oh sure," Chase scoffed, "if I want to see my son two, maybe three times a year, then I suppose I do. There are other considerations as well."

"Would one of those happen to be Jo Benoit?" Matthew suggested.

"That's something I keep asking myself." Chase didn't even try to evade the question. "I don't suppose I have to tell you that I love her."

"No"—his father chuckled—"you don't. But," he went on in a more serious vein, "have you taken into consideration the responsibility that will come with the baby? With marriage? I assume you are thinking of marriage? There's something else you've got to think about as well. Neither Jo, nor any woman for that matter, is likely to be thrilled if you decide at some future date that you suddenly aren't content with coming home each evening."

Chase stared at his father, annoyance clearly stamped on his granite features. "You do believe in bringing it all out into the open, don't you?"

"Do you disagree?"

"No, I don't disagree," Chase said slowly. Contrary to what his thoughts had been only weeks before, he found the prospect of a future with Jo to be far more enticing than waking up in some remote spot on the globe and fighting dust and flies. Suddenly a wry grin pulled at his lips. He regarded his father thoughtfully. "Have you noticed a resemblance between Mom and Jo—in the way they think, that is?"

"Oh, yes." Matthew nodded. "I was wondering when you'd mention that. Are you perhaps thinking that in a few months or years you'll be ready for a padded cell?"

"Something like that," Chase replied, frowning. "How the hell have you managed? There are times, with Jo when I haven't the slightest idea what she's talking about. We'll be discussing one thing, and without one word of warning, she'll take off on something entirely different."

197

"Don't worry about it. In time, you'll find yourself a master at unraveling her conversations, even her erratic trains of thought. There's a lot to be said for women like your mother and Jo, Chase." Matthew shrugged. "Life is never boring with them, and"—he grinned smugly—"after a few years, you'll find you've started to think like them as well."

"God forbid!" Chase shuddered. "It's like living half your life in the Twilight Zone."

"I'll have you know," Matthew said sternly, "the Twilight Zone is a hell of a nice place to be with a woman like your mother."

"I'm sure it is, Dad." But later, after Matthew was back in his own office and Chase had a few minutes to himself, he wondered if he would ever get used to Jo and her erratic thinking.

Certainly you will, his conscience assured him. Look at your parents. They've been together forty-odd years. Do you know of a happier couple? There's also one small detail you've overlooked. You haven't asked Jo to marry you, and she hasn't accepted. Aren't you just a wee bit ahead of yourself?

Chase stared into space as he fought against the thought of her refusal. Suddenly he had the strongest urge to rush right over to Jo's and propose. Don't be an ass, the same wily conscience mocked him. The woman's pregnant, for heaven's sake. At this precise moment, marriage is the farthest thing from her mind. She's clumsy, she doesn't feel well, and she definitely doesn't need some yo-yo jumping from behind the bushes waving a ring in front of her nose.

With a not-so-steady hand, brought on by the realization that he could possibly lose Jo, Chase picked up the material Laura had given him and tried to concentrate on the mysterious job. At least that was something he could be successful with, he told himself. A new gleam of determination surfaced in his eyes as he reached for the phone. A good fight was what he needed, and he knew exactly how to go about getting it started. It was time that pimply-faced kid at Overton's was taught a lesson, and there was no doubt in Chase's mind that he was the man to do the teaching!

CHAPTER FIFTEEN

"You're bored," Mary Clare told Jo. They were on their way to the small office where Personal Touch Greeting Cards was located. Mary Clare had called and offered to pick up Jo, rather than have her wrestle with the stick shift of the VW. "The nursery is ready, the baby has enough clothes to outfit triplets, and you have time on your hands."

"I really shouldn't have done it, you know," Jo fretted. "But he made me so darn angry."

Mary Clare, always a little startled when Jo let loose with some left-field remark, frantically searched her mind for some inkling as to what this latest statement pertained to. She'd known Jo for years. They were close friends. But somehow she'd never been able to grasp the workings of her friend's mind.

The baby. She had to be talking about the baby. "Blaming yourself for what happened isn't going to do any good, honey. You should try to put that behind you now. After all, Lance was so much stronger than you. Just be thankful you weren't hurt."

"It was as though I had no say in the matter at all."

"From all accounts, that's the way those things usually go," Mary Clare assured her. "I'm sure you couldn't have stopped it from happening."

"Actually, the little blue one was nicer and would have been far easier to handle. I wouldn't have had to fuss with the stick shift," Jo prattled on.

"What 'little blue one'? What are you talking about?" a bewildered Mary Clare asked. They were stopped at a traffic light and she was staring at Jo in confusion.

Jo, equally perplexed, looked questioningly at her friend. "You're not making much sense, Mary Clare. Haven't you been listening to me?"

Mary Clare placed a palm on either side of her head and pressed her temples gently. "Jo, darling," she murmured in a determined effort to prove she wasn't going crazy, "let's begin again. What is it you shouldn't have done?"

"Why, Mary Clare, it's simple. I shouldn't have bought the VW. If I had listened to Chase, you wouldn't have had to pick me up today, and I wouldn't feel as though I'm wrestling a bear each time I go to the grocery store."

"Oh."

"Aren't you feeling well today? Your mind seems to be wandering."

"I thought I was feeling super."

"Ahh well, don't fret," Jo assured her. "Love has a way of doing that to people."

"Love? What are you talking about?" Mary Clare asked suspiciously.

"Long periods of daydreaming, the inability to comprehend the simplest of problems. It won't last forever."

"That's comforting to know." Mary Clare didn't try to explain. Why bother? Jo was in one of her moods, and when that was the case, explanations served little purpose. "I'm sure Mo will be glad to hear that as well. He's been very forgetful lately."

"Good." Jo beamed, her hands demurely clasped over her rotund tummy. "Now that the two of you are finally talking to each other instead of shouting, I'm positive good things will come of the relationship."

"Such as?" Mary Clare asked skeptically.

"Marriage, babies—I would suspect Mo is a very virile man, Mary Clare, but I'm sure you already know that. I can see you now, with three or four little boys following like stairsteps. Need I say more?"

"No!" a pale Mary Clare exclaimed. She turned into the parking lot behind the building where their business was located and screeched to a stop. What had started out as a beautiful day had suddenly turned into a nightmare.

When Jo and Mary Clare entered the pleasantly

decorated workroom, they found a red-faced Carla being teased by Mo Tyson.

"How nice," Jo exclaimed, favoring the large man with a bright smile. "We were just talking about you." Carla, relieved at being rescued, quickly shot to her desk in the corner of the room and sat down.

Mo looked from Jo to a rigid-faced Mary Clare, and put two and two together in a hurry. "I need to go over this last phase of Harry's contract with you, Mary Clare," he said smoothly. "Do you have a few minutes?" The tall blonde nodded, then led the way into the minuscule office used by all three of them from time to time.

Jo walked over to Carla's desk and handed her the rough layouts for the latest cards they were adding to their line.

Carla looked at each of the drawings, nodding from time to time. "These are fantastic, Jo. And the detail is amazing. How on earth did you find time to get through these so quickly?"

"I'm hardly the belle of the ball this season, or haven't you noticed?" she asked pertly, patting her tummy. "My phone has been strangely quiet from most of my former suitors. Can you imagine?"

"You're a nut." Carla blushed. "But seriously, you shouldn't push yourself so hard."

"I didn't push myself," Jo told her. "My work keeps me from being bored."

"By the way, I saw this yesterday and thought

you'd like it," Carla murmured as she reached into a drawer and withdrew a light-blue bag. "I suppose you can tell from what's inside that I hope it's a girl," she added shyly.

Jo smiled as she opened the bag and removed the most gorgeous tiny pink dress she'd ever seen. Even to someone such as she, who could barely sew on a button, it was plain to see the tiny garment was handmade. "It's beautiful, Carla. Please tell me you didn't almost put your eyes out sewing these tiny stitches."

"Nonsense. You know I'm always having to redress my doll collection, so tiny stitches are nothing. Besides, this baby is special. Why shouldn't she have the best?"

"She?" Jo laughed.

"She," Carla said determinedly.

So far the sides were about equal, Jo mused. She had enough clothes for a boy or a girl. Two evenings ago, while Chase was setting up the crib and she was putting away the clothes that kept arriving, he had made the remark—jokingly—that she should have twins. Her "Mind your own business" had made him laugh and tell her that he was doing just that. Jo had chosen not to probe the seemingly harmless remark. The vibes she'd been getting lately from Chase were entirely different from those during the first few months of their relationship. She was a coward not to press him, she supposed, but neither did she want to be hurt.

When Mo and Mary Clare came out of the office a few minutes later, Jo saw the rosy glow that accented her friend's features and smiled. Mo was coming around just as she'd known he would. Wouldn't it be nice, Jo thought to herself, if in a few months time Carla could create a tiny pink dress for Mary Clare?

"You're looking mighty pleased with yourself," Mo teased Jo. He dropped an arm across her shoulders and gave her a quick hug. "How's the brat these days?"

"Kicking like crazy," she said with a sigh.

"That's because the kid needs some headroom. You're so small, he's boxed in," Mo informed her as if he were an authority on the subject. He glanced down at her rounded figure and shook his massive head. "If something doesn't give pretty soon, kid, I do believe you will explode."

"How delicately put!" Mary Clare hooted.

"But very true," Carla agreed. "Have you spoken to Jo about this evening?"

"Not yet," Mary Clare hedged.

"What about this evening?" Mo frowned suspiciously. He looked at all three women, their faces as unrevealing as a sphinx. "Okay," he said with a growl, "I can take a hint. But remember, if you get into trouble, don't call me."

After he'd gone, Jo was told that she was being invited out for the evening.

"By whom?"

"The two of us." Mary Clare waved toward Carla. "You wouldn't let us give you a baby shower, so we decided to take you out for an evening on the town. We'll pick you up at six-thirty for dinner. Then"—she gestured expressively with her hands—"who knows what will happen?"

"What do you mean, you don't know when you'll be back?" Chase demanded, his granite chin thrust forward and his eyes stormy. To make matters worse, he was standing smack in the middle of Jo's bedroom, and every time she moved, she had to step around him.

"I'm going out, as I've already explained, with Carla and Mary Clare. I don't know where we're going or when we'll be home," Jo patiently explained for the third or fourth time. She looked at Chase in the mirror and grinned. "I suppose you could call this evening my swansong, whatever that's supposed to mean." She ran a smoothing hand over her dark, lustrous hair, then stepped back and critically eyed her dress. "What do you think?"

"I think it's lousy," Chase remarked glumly.

"Really? I think it's nice. It only makes me look plump as opposed to what I really look like."

"I was referring to your plans for the evening, not the dress. That color red is very good for you. You look beautiful," he said bleakly.

"Thank you. What about you?" Jo asked. "Do you have plans for the evening?"

"Nothing exciting, I'm afraid. I brought home some work from the office." Christ! He was behaving like a damned fool. There was nothing in the world wrong with Jo going out with her friends for the evening. He'd told himself that at least fifty times in the last ten minutes. But saying it and believing it were not the same thing. What it boiled down to, he finally admitted, was that he was jealous as hell of her family, of Mary Clare, Carla, Mo, and any other of her friends who took up a second of her time.

"Are you sure you feel like going out this evening?" he finally broke the uneasy silence.

"I feel fine. Don't worry," Jo scolded him gently and reached up to pat his cheek. "I'm not so fragile that I'll break if you aren't there to look after me."

Chase reached for her then, his arms going around her, his hands locking behind her back. "You are notorious for not taking care of yourself, Ms. Benoit," he said huskily. "You take unnecessary risks, and you look at the world through rose-colored glasses."

"You worry too much," Jo said softly, wanting to believe what she saw revealed in his eyes, but her inner voice of reasoning added its own caution. The rapid beat of his heart could be felt against the sensitive tips of her fingers spread against the solid wall of his chest. "Worry causes lines here"—she lightly traced the outer edges of his eyes—"and here"—letting the pad of her thumb rest against the corner of his bottom lip.

"Lines of that nature are supposed to make me look distinguished," Chase murmured, his head dipping so that his lips could feather the inviting line of her mouth.

"How unfair," Jo whispered, her voice trembling. "On a woman's face they're called wrinkles," she continued as her mouth opened to the gentle urgency he'd awakened in her.

His hands ran swiftly and possessively over her back, and the combined shock waves of fire and ice ran from her toes to the top of her head. Hot—cold—the first beckoning her further into a world of velvet darkness and ecstasy, the bonds slipping effortlessly in place about her. Yet the other was more cautious, the restraints like manacles of steel binding her to an unsure future.

It was the combined sound of the doorbell and the kicking of the baby that broke the spell and released Jo from the overpowering magic of Chase's embrace.

"I've got to go," she whispered. Her hands pushed against the wall of muscle that burned through the material of his shirt and scorched her fingertips.

"You don't *have* to go," Chase corrected her, though he made no effort to detain her. His hands gripped her shoulders for a moment, then slid like a whisper down her arms to catch her hands.

"I want to go," Jo said, as though she needed those words to put some space between them. In Chase's arms she'd found something she wasn't capable of handling just then. It had been there before, an elusive, shimmering desire that pulled at her, but frightened her as well.

Chase stared at her for a long moment, then released her hands and stepped back. He turned and reached for the small black clutch bag and placed it in her hands. "You'll be needing this."

"Yes, thank you," Jo murmured, avoiding the brooding watchfulness of his gaze.

The fourth member of the party was to meet them at the restaurant. Jo was rendered speechless when she saw Elise waving at them from the table they were making their way to.

"Elise?" Jo whispered to Mary Clare in a moment of panic.

"In the flesh," Mary Clare quipped. "Just for the heck of it, I decided to call her. You're no more surprised than I was when she accepted."

By then they were at the table and the waiter was scrambling to seat Jo, his expression showing plainly that he expected her to give birth during the main course.

"Don't worry." She patted his hand reassuringly. "I promise to be a good girl and not disrupt your evening."

"Thank you, madam," the solemn-faced waiter intoned in a relieved voice. He placed menus before each of them, then melted into the background, a terrified man.

"This is quite a surprise." Jo turned and smiled at her sister. "I wasn't aware that you knew Mary Clare or Carla."

"I didn't," Elise said awkwardly, "but when Mary Clare called last week and told me about this evening, it sounded like fun. I dropped by the office later and introduced myself."

After that small hurdle had been passed, everyone began talking at the same time. After her initial shock of seeing Elise—an Elise who was soon laughing and talking as animatedly as the others—Jo relaxed and let the gay mood of the evening slip over her. If in the back of her mind she was thinking of Chase and feeling the loss of his arms around her, she hid it perfectly. Her relationship with him was too precious, too fragile, for her to allow it to become a topic of discussion.

After dinner and two very small glasses of wine, which made Jo feel remarkably wobbly-legged, the party moved on toward the entertainment phase of the evening.

An unsteady Jo, flanked on either side by a slightly tipsy Elise and a laughing Mary Clare, looked up at the brightly lighted facade of the establishment they were about to enter. "I've never been to this place. Do you suppose there'll be droves of handsome men in there who will try to pick us up?"

"The eternal optimist," Carla warbled as she steadfastly tried to maneuver the door and her purse and Jo's. "The last thing you need worry about is being picked up by a man. What would you do with him, for heaven's sake?"

"Have him stuffed and mounted," Jo said brightly. "That way I'd always have a ready model."

"I don't think Mother would like that." Elise shook her head decisively. "She wouldn't like that at all. You'd better dress him in something. . . . How about a towel?"

"Good idea." Jo nodded. She leaned back and stared at her sister. "You know, Elise, you're not half bad. I should have taken you out much sooner."

The arrival of another large group helped their progress inside. They made their way to a small table close to a circular area Jo assumed to be the dance floor.

One thing did strike her as odd, however, in spite of the wine. "There is definitely something wrong with this place," she hissed to her three companions as they settled around the table and ordered drinks from the handsome young waiter.

211

"How so?" Mary Clare asked, her eyes dancing with amusement.

"So far I've spotted only half a dozen or so men. Men, the opposite sex, m-a-l-e. Do you get my drift?"

"Don't worry, you—" Mary Clare's explanation was abruptly cut off by the sound of a drum roll and the appearance into the middle of the "dance floor" of a character in a tuxedo, sporting the longest handlebar moustache Jo had ever seen.

"Ladies and"—he smirked at the few men present—"gentlemen. Welcome to the Club Eros."

Jo turned and stared disbelievingly at her three friends, who were giving the man on the stage their undivided attention. "Did you hear what he called this place?" she whispered.

"Shhh." Carla poked her with her elbow. "I don't want to miss anything."

"What on earth could you possibly miss?" the still unsuspecting Jo asked. She propped an elbow onto the edge of the table and leaned her forehead against her hand. "I can't believe you've brought me to a strip joint!"

"But it's not just any strip joint," Mary Clare murmured in her ear. "Take a look at that gorgeous hunk of man coming out."

Jo slowly raised her head, her gray eyes almost bulging from their sockets as they focused on the tall, tanned, blond man who had halted in the center of the dance floor. He snapped his head forward with such force, and at such an uncomfortable angle, Jo was certain she could hear the crack of bones. One hand was thrust in the pocket of the sleeveless black leather vest, holding the garment open to reveal a chest with only a sprinkling of fine hair. The other hand was resting on the ornate buckle of the silver belt looped through the low-slung fit of the incredibly tight leather pants he was wearing.

The crowded audience stared mesmerized as the young man began to gyrate his hips in perfect sync with the beat of the music. When the hand at his waist flipped open the buckle and pulled the belt from the pants loops, the audience sprang to life. Jo watched dazed as the belt was tossed into the sea of waving hands.

The beat of the music increased. The movements of the dancer became more suggestive. When the vest came slithering down his muscular arms, a number of the women actually left their seats and rushed to the edge of the stage. The vest was royally bestowed upon a laughing brunette. Instead of returning to her seat, however, the brunette remained standing where she was.

When one slim hand of the performer teased at the zipper of the leather pants, the roar of the crowd was deafening. To her own amazement, Jo joined in. In all her twenty-seven years, she decided, she'd never seen anything like this, and she didn't intend missing a single minute of it. When the black leather pants were finally removed and tossed into the crowd, Jo simply closed her eyes and shook her head. The string bikini briefs left little to the imagination, and at that precise moment, Jo's imagination was in overdrive!

CHAPTER SIXTEEN

Jo heard the sound of someone moving around in the kitchen and groaned. Damn Elise! Staying over was one thing. Getting up before daylight on Saturday morning was something else.

The noise of a cupboard door being slammed, then reopened and slammed again, made Jo's gray eyes turn to steely points of anger. She threw back the covers, pushed herself to the edge of the bed and eventually to her feet. Without donning slippers or robe, she padded on bare feet from her room, down the hall, and into the kitchen, her dark hair tousled and her otherwise smooth forehead showing definite creases of anger.

"Will you please tell me just what the hell is going on in here?" she demanded as she rounded the dividing bar and burst into the kitchen. But it wasn't Elise who was making enough racket to awaken the dead. It was Chase.

He was down on his haunches, scrambling blithely through a lower cupboard. "Good morning," he greeted over his shoulder in a sickeningly bright voice. "I'm looking for a larger skillet. I'm in the mood for pancakes with my eggs, and that dinky thing you use isn't big enough to cook a gnat in."

"I like cooking gnats!" Jo stormed at him. "I also like peace and quiet when I wake up in the mornings!" God! Her head felt as big as a pumpkin.

Chase found the skillet he wanted, then stood up. He surveyed her critically and then shook his head. "You look like hell."

"I feel like hell," Jo retorted, snarling. "Now can you possibly put those two points together and realize that I'm not in the mood for company?"

"You need to eat." Chase grinned at her, unruffled by her lousy temper. "Did you have a nice time last night?" he asked innocently. He opened the refrigerator and began taking out bacon and eggs and all the other trappings for the morning meal.

Jo's stomach turned at the thought of eating. "I'm not hungry."

"You will be." He kept on working unperturbed. "Scrambled or fried?"

She closed her eyes and groaned. "Make it scrambled, to match your brain. What time is it anyway?"

"Eight-thirty. Why?"

"It can't be. It's still dark outside."

"Cloudy. We're in for a bad storm."

216

"Oh." Jo turned away, then paused. "You'd better make enough for three. I have company."

"Who?" Chase swiveled around and stared hard at her.

"Elise," she said over her shoulder as she left the room.

Jo was bent over the sink in the bathroom, splashing her face with handful after handful of water, when she felt Chase's presence behind her. Her psychic powers weren't really that good, she admitted irritably, considering that the jarring thud of her bedroom door as it banged against the wall could be heard at least a block away.

"Why has your sister suddenly decided to babysit you?" The scowling countenance of her protector appeared in the mirror beside her own dripping face.

"Perhaps word's gotten out that I'm being kept prisoner by a mean-tempered, overbearing, obnoxious ass," she said sweetly, the thin smile on her lips doing little to soften the storm gathering in her gray eyes. Jo hurried around the intimidating mountain raining frigid disapproval down upon her head and entered her adjoining bedroom.

"What on earth was that awful commotion I just heard?" Elise asked as she came hurrying into the bedroom. "I could have sworn I heard voices." She was clad in an old threadbare T-shirt of Jo's that barely covered the tops of her thighs. Her dark hair was standing in dark, silky puffs about

217

her face, and Jo knew at that moment, she'd never seen her sister look so alive.

"Er . . . just a neighbor wanting to borrow some milk," Jo lied without batting an eye. If Chase didn't keep his behind in that bathroom until she got Elise back to her room, Jo knew she would kill him. An evening of watching male strippers was one thing. Elise would never in a million years buy the story that she and Chase were just friends. Jo took a couple of steps backward, motioning frantically with the hand held behind her for Chase to keep quiet. "Why don't you go back to bed? It's early yet. I'll fix some breakfast later and call you."

"Sleep?" Elise smiled with all the pleasure of a cat licking its whiskers after a nice saucer of milk. "Who can possibly think of sleeping after that . . . remarkable evening we spent?" She walked over and dropped onto Jo's bed, then sprawled back. "Can you imagine what Mother would say if she knew her two daughters had spent the better part of last evening yelling and screaming for men to take off their clothes?"

"What the hell do you mean by that crack?" Chase barreled into the room like a shot from a cannon.

Elise gave a startled scream and grabbed the sheet, holding it against her chest for dear life.

Jo calmly observed the two intruders in her bedroom and proceeded to brush her hair.

"Well?" a near-snarling Chase demanded of Elise, who was staring at him with the same horror one would regard an approaching tiger. "Just what the hell do you mean, you and your sister were begging men to take off their clothes?"

"Jo?" Elise's voice quavered imploringly.

Her sister gave her a helpless look. "This is Chase," she murmured with a faint shrug.

"You!" Chase took a menacing step toward the bed, one long finger pointed at Elise. "I want an explanation from you. Your sister is a master at clouding the issue. Now talk!"

"You—you really—sh-should try to calm down. Emotional stress is very bad for you. Besides, I've never seen such a . . . er . . . display in my entire life," Elise murmured faintly.

"I'm sure there must be some deep-seated exhibitionist syndrome hidden in you somewhere," Jo said calmly as she pulled the brush through her hair.

"I suppose I'm sorry for that," Elise said thoughtfully, "but it was interesting all the same."

"I don't believe it." Chase slowly shook his head, his expression icy. "You're as daffy as your sister. What the hell are you talking about?" he yelled.

"Stop yelling!" Elise fired right back.

"Please excuse me," Chase cracked mockingly. "I do humbly apologize for seeming the least bit concerned. Why"—he included both sisters in the fiery glance that seemed to peel paint from the walls—"I can't imagine why your waltzing in and calmly announcing how you enjoyed yelling and screaming for men to strip should arouse my curiosity, can you?"

"Put like that, I can see how you might be due an explanation." Elise shot Jo an imploring glance. Receiving nothing but total vagueness from that sector, she had no recourse but to muddle through as best she could. "We decided to treat Jo to a night on the town last night."

"I know," Chase snapped. "Dinner, perhaps a movie—or so I was led to believe. Where did you wind up?"

"The Club Eros. Have you ever been there?" Elise asked nervously. "You should go sometime. It's the most remarkable place I've ever seen."

Chase ran a hand over his face, rapidly blinking his eyes in an attempt to clear his head. He stared from Elise to Jo, his expression so comically angry both were tempted to laugh, but thought better of the idea. "You actually took your pregnant sister, due to deliver in less than a week, to a sleazy dive like the Club Eros?"

"Then you *have* been there?" Elise brightened considerably. "Did you catch the tanned, black-haired guy's act? I caught the beaded ornament attached to his—his—" She turned to a transfixed Jo. "What do you call those cute little things they all wore? Couldn't be called g-strings, could they?"

About the only comforting thought to pass through Jo's mind as she endured Chase's fierce gaze was the rather pleasant realization that Elise was truly her sister. Wouldn't Sarah Kincaid be surprised to know she'd failed twice? But before she had time to really savor the moment, Chase turned on his heel and stormed from the room.

Elise stared at the doorway, then turned and looked at Jo. "I can't tell you how sorry I am." She sighed and shook her head. "Last night something snapped in me. For years—no, all my life, I've lived my life exactly as Mother dictated. Never questioning, never arguing."

Jo walked over and sat on the edge of the bed and then reached out to pat Elise's hand, which was still gripping the sheet. "It's all right."

"No, it isn't," Elise said quietly. "I've made Chase angry at you because I couldn't keep my mouth shut." She gave a harsh little laugh. "Can you imagine that? Me, Elise Kincaid, successful stockbroker, noted for my professionalism, babbling like an idiot."

"Don't put yourself down," Jo said sternly. "You haven't done anything wrong. Chase will cool down before long and be right back over here ordering me about. He's like that. As for letting your hair down, then I'm afraid I can't do anything there but encourage you. I was so glad to see you do it. I've lived in awe of you for as long as I can remember. You've always been perfect. It's

221

nice to know there's a thoroughly human side to you after all."

"You've lived in awe of me?" Elise asked in a stunned voice. "That's incredible." She ducked her head, her fingers plucking nervously at the sheet. "I've always been in awe of *you* and how independent you are. Remember all those outrageous things you used to do when you were growing up?" Jo nodded. "Well, I was always behind you—in thought only, I'm afraid—but behind you. You've always had the courage to fight Mother's iron control. You never let her take over your life. I suppose you could say I've always been a little jealous of you."

"Well, sister dear, listening to us talk leaves me with only one conclusion. We've both been incredibly stupid," Jo said flatly. "We've wasted some precious years going our separate ways, when all we had to do was talk to each other, really talk and listen to what the other was saying."

"I agree." Elise smiled. "Though I'm not sure how Mother will take our becoming friends."

"Don't worry about it," Jo said lightly. She pushed herself to her feet, then looked back at Elise and grinned. "It will be rather nice having another maverick in the family." Though judging from Chase's reaction, she wasn't sure he could put up with *two* dopey females!

Jake looked up from the dough he was pounding, his bushy brows drawn together in annoyance. "Do you mind?" he snapped at Chase, who had reduced the neat kitchen to a shambles in less than thirty minutes. There were three glasses on the counter, along with a plate, a knife, and a fork. The stove now boasted a greasy film from the bacon Chase had fried. "I make bread when I want to relax, but you"—he waved a flour-dusted hand —"you make a damn mess. What exactly is your problem?"

Chase whirled around from his pacing, his face a rigid mask of disapproval. "Can you believe she actually went to a male strip joint last night?"

"I assume you mean Jo?"

"Hell yes, I mean Jo! She was accompanied on her evening's tour by that addlepated sister of hers and her two partners. She's eight and a half months pregnant, for Christ's sake!"

"So?"

"So?" Chase bellowed. "What do you mean so? She could have been hurt in that screaming crowd of females, all yelling for some damn weirdos to take off their clothes!"

"Sounds like innocent fun," Jake told him, not in the least shocked.

"You're sick," Chase glowered.

"No, I'm being reasonable," Jake corrected him, "something I'd advise you to start doing."

"What the hell is that supposed to mean?"

"You aren't Jo's keeper, Chase. She doesn't need a jailer telling her when to breathe, when to eat, or where she can or cannot go. She managed quite nicely before you took over her life."

"What you're really saying is that she doesn't need me at all, isn't it?" Some of the fire had gone out of Chase, replaced by the cold hand of fear gripping his heart. Jo did need him, he kept repeating to himself, she had to.

"I wouldn't go that far." For once Jake softened his tone of voice. He saw the pain in Chase's face, and compassion welled up inside him for the younger man. He'd been with Chase for a long time, and he cared for him. Chase and Bink were his family, and he would go to any lengths to protect them. "Jo is not like the other women you've known. She's independent and used to going her own way. Right now she's vulnerable, and her condition is causing her to act differently than she normally would. You've been here to help her, and that's good. But it still doesn't give you the right to run her life, Chase. And once the baby is born, she'll not want you hovering over her."

"I don't hover," Chase said shortly. "It's just that she's so damned irresponsible. When I think of her trying to take care of herself and a baby, I become terrified, Jake. I've never felt like that before."

"Love does that to people, Chase."

"Am I that transparent?"

224

"Unfortunately, yes." Jake continued kneading the dough, a smirky little grin softening his weathered face. "I've watched this whole thing from the beginning. You put up a damn good fight, my friend, but the widow Benoit has tied you in more knots than a rodeo rider with a snarled lasso."

Chase muttered an oath and swung around to storm out of the room just as the telephone rang. He walked over to the counter and snatched up the receiver. "Hello?" he barked.

"Chase? Alex Grenwyck. How's the world treating you?"

"Like hell, Alex. And you?"

"Tolerable."

"Where are you?" Chase asked, excitement creeping into him at hearing his old friend's voice. He hadn't spoken to Alex since the last "job" they had done in Central America. Alex was part of his past, a past that had been exciting, dangerous, filled with intrigue. A past that had no place for pregnant women with gray eyes and hair as black as midnight.

"I'm in Houston. Got in late last night. How about meeting me for lunch?"

"Name the place."

An hour and a half later Chase was entering the dining room of a local motel, headed for the table at the rear where he saw Alex sitting reading a paper.

225

"Is this how you spend your Saturday mornings now?" he quipped as he reached the table.

Alex looked up, a smile breaking the tired planes of his face. He stood, caught Chase's outstretched hand and gripped it hard. "It's good to see you. Sit down. How about some coffee?"

"Sounds good." Chase nodded as he pulled out a chair. "What do you mean by staying at a motel? You had my number, you should have come out to the house."

"I had several calls to make when I got in, so I thought it best to stay here. I'll take you up on that offer another time." After pouring a cup of coffee and pushing it toward Chase, Alex sat back, his shrewd gaze studying his friend. "How's it feel being the executive?"

Chase grinned ruefully. "I'm adjusting. Actually, it beats the hell out of eating a pound of dust a day and living off bad food."

"And Bink? How's he doing?"

"Fine. Growing like a weed. I'll soon have a teenager on my hands. Can you believe that?"

"No. And I prefer not to dwell on it either. It makes me feel old."

They both laughed, and the conversation turned to past exploits. After reliving the highlights of their ten-year relationship, Chase got the distinct feeling Alex was leading up to something. He brought the matter to a head by asking him outright.

"I thought I was being subtle." Alex grinned sheepishly.

"Not when you keep going on about the good old days," Chase remarked dryly. "We didn't have *that* many good ones. We had some fun, sure. But the danger involved was always there as well. What's on your mind?"

"I need your help."

"I'm retired, remember?"

"I haven't forgotten, but this job needs your special touch, Chase."

"You'd better explain, then we'll decide how much good my special 'touch' will do."

"We've had one of the biggest security leaks in years. Fortunately the individual working on this end was apprehended, but the information is already on its way. Our only recourse at this point is to try to intercept the microfilm before it leaves Mexico."

"Mexico?" Chase asked. "Why there?"

"That's where the exchange is supposed to go down. There's a double agent hanging out there who's willing to help us for a price."

"I'll bet."

"Don't scoff." Alex shrugged. "At the moment, it's the best we can do."

"How do I fit into all this?"

"We want you to go to Mexico as Chase Colbern, private citizen, representing Colbern Engineering. At some point during the first few hours of your visit, you will be contacted by a Mr. Garcia. He's on our side. If all goes as planned, you should have the microfilm in your hands within forty-eight hours of your arrival. You'll pass the microfilm to me and then—after you've met with perfectly innocent individuals about the construction of a dam to provide irrigation for a drought-stricken area—you'll return to Houston."

"Sounds simple enough. How long should all this take?"

"Five days at the most. We want it to look like a legitimate business trip. Your ability in the past to come and go under the protection of your company is of vital importance. That's another reason for your staying on in Mexico for a couple of days. So far we've no reason to believe your cover has been blown, and we'd like to keep it that way. We don't want your family singled out as kidnap victims by some radical group backed by the enemy."

"How soon do you need an answer?" Chase asked.

"Yesterday." Alex sighed. "This thing only broke a couple of days ago. So far we've been able to keep it from the press. As you know, there've been a number of devastating leaks lately. It doesn't look good for our side, and the administration is mad as hell. There is one little thing I left out."

"Such as?"

"You'll need a wife. Remember Lucy Bouder?"

"Two years ago in Caracas. Sexy brunette, right?" Chase grinned. "But why a wife?"

"Two reasons. Lucy's a damned good agent, plus we need to pad the act. What could be more believable than a wife following her husband to Mexico for a mini-vacation?"

"When would I need to leave?"

"Tonight. Lucy will fly into Houston tonight. Tomorrow afternoon she'll use tickets issued in the name of Mrs. Chase Colbern and join her husband in Mexico." Alex reached into his inside jacket pocket and removed an envelope. He handed it to Chase. "You'll find everything is in perfect order. Tickets, reservations, the works."

Chase was of two minds as he ran the tip of his finger over the edge of the envelope. He'd thought this phase of his life was finished. Yet he couldn't deny the adrenaline pumping through his veins as he listened to Alex explain the setup. He'd lived on excitement for years, and he could feel it creeping into him again, urging him to go . . . go.

Why not? he argued with himself. Bink would be safe with Jake. His family was unaware of the double life he'd led and wouldn't worry unduly. That left Jo. Perhaps Jake had been right, Chase mused in those few moments of silence. Perhaps he had been too protective of her. Maybe a few days apart would give them both a different perspective. Surely Jo wouldn't be in any danger of having the baby in that short amount of time? It was a risk, he admitted, but it was one risk he knew he had to take. He wanted more with Jo than simply being the man next door . . . even her lover next door. He wanted a life with her—he wanted to marry her.

Chase raised the cup of coffee toward Alex and smiled. "To Mexico."

CHAPTER SEVENTEEN

"Is that all he said, Jake?" Jo asked as she sat in the Colbern kitchen. She reached for the cup of coffee Jake set before her, her expression troubled. "He didn't say why he had to leave so hurriedly?"

"All he had on his mind was some blasted dam," Jake replied, frowning. He pulled up a chair with the tip of his shoe and sat down. "He said good-bye to Bink. And he did try to find you. I will give him credit for that. How about a piece of that chocolate cake I just made?" he asked persuasively.

"No." Jo shook her head. "I'm afraid I'm not hungry. After we finished shopping, Elise and I had a hamburger. Now I wish I hadn't gone out at all. That way I would have been here to see Chase."

"Stop worrying." Jake patted her hand. "You know Chase. Always running off here and there. He'll be back before you know it." But in his own mind, Jake wasn't so sure. There was something mighty strange about this latest trip. There'd been that call from Alex Grenwyck, after which Chase shot out of the house. When he returned home later in the afternoon, he'd begun throwing things in a suitcase, talking about some dam in Mexico. Something wasn't right, but Jake was at a loss to figure it out.

"Did you buy a lot of things for the baby?" he asked, hoping to take Jo's mind off worrying about Chase. Damn fool! Jake fumed. There was no cause to worry the poor girl like this, no cause at all.

"Actually, my sister did most of the buying." Jo smiled. "If I hadn't complained of being tired, we would still be walking from store to store."

"It's nice for you and Elise to be friends."

"Yes, it is. We did a lot of talking this morning. It's amazing how two people can go for years at cross-purposes with each other, then suddenly realize how much alike they really are."

"Well, it's good that you finally worked out your differences. What does she think of Chase?" Jake asked with a chuckle.

"I don't think she's ever met anyone quite like him. This morning"—Jo briefly closed her eyes and shuddered—"he was like a raving maniac, and all poor Elise could do was confess everything we did last night. I think about the only thing she left out was the wine I drank. I'm certain if Chase had continued his own special brand of interrogation, she'd have blurted that out as well."

232

She pushed back her chair and rose to her feet. "I really must go, Jake. If you hear anything from Chase, let me know. Okay?"

"Will do. And if you need me during the night, just call me on that contraption Chase hooked up," the older man said gruffly. "Come on." He tucked her hand in the crook of his arm. "I'll see you to your door. And don't worry about that little noise you heard in the VW. I was in charge of the motor pool when I retired from the army. There's not an engine been made that I can't fix. I'll leave it parked in our garage till you need it tomorrow. How does that sound?"

"Sounds great, Jake. I won't be going out until around eleven in the morning. Mary Clare has invited me over for brunch—in case you hear anything," she tacked on.

Once inside her own house, Jo found herself unable to settle down. She tried to read, but the words made no sense. She finally threw down the book in frustration. Television, a succession of reruns, offered little in the way of entertainment. Her mind was on Chase, and nothing she did deterred her thoughts.

She'd been completely shocked when Jake had given her the news that Chase was gone. There were so many things she wanted to tell him, things she wanted to explain. She wanted to share her reunion with Elise with him. To some, that might not be important, but Chase would understand. He

233

would probably make some teasing remark, but he'd understand. The VW was making a peculiar noise, and she'd meant to mention it to him. There was also the drawer in the nursery closet that was sticking. Chase had warned her it might happen, but said not to worry, he would fix it.

Listen to yourself, she thought with a sigh, dropping her head back against the sofa. Your entire life is entangled with Chase. No, it isn't, she argued back, but it was wasted effort on her part. He *was* a part of her now. He lived in her thoughts and her heart in a way that brought tears to her eyes. She hadn't even been home to tell him goodbye.

The remainder of the evening passed with the dullness of an aching tooth. When exhaustion finally did bring on sleep, her dreams were riddled with images of Chase. She saw him in every conceivable situation, from an angry outburst to an exhibition at the Club Eros, gyrating his hips to the beat of the music while he stripped to the delight of the yelling, screaming women.

The next morning Jo woke with a splitting headache. After a long lecture on the sins of lying in bed when she wasn't really ill, she forced herself to get up and staggered to the bathroom. Sometime later, fortified by a long, soothing shower, she began to dress. She'd promised to be at Mary Clare's for brunch, though at the moment all she wanted was to crawl back into bed. She had a pretty good

234

idea Mary Clare's brunch was to be a continuation of the celebration from the previous night. Jo shuddered. Friends were wonderful, and she adored hers, but their plans for helping her through her last boring days of pregnancy were beginning to pall.

The VW started without a hitch. The troublesome noise had disappeared as suddenly as it had begun. Bless Jake's heart, Jo thought with a sigh as she backed carefully out of the Colbern driveway. Maybe it wouldn't happen again. That would prevent her from having to endure the smug I-told-you-so look on Chase's face.

Don't kid yourself, her conscience jeered. How do you know you'll ever see any expression on Chase's face again? It just might be, Ms. Benoit, that your neighbor has tired of playing nursemaid to you. He may have had enough. What would you do then? The thought was so disquieting, Jo slammed on the brakes to keep from hitting a large dark car broadside as it made a turn in front of her.

But wait. That car ran the stop sign, not you. As she shifted the VW into first gear and began to move forward again, she glanced into the rearview mirror. The car she'd almost struck had turned around and was directly behind her. Must be lost, Jo decided. But lost or not, the driver seemed to be a complete idiot. The car pulled out and drew alongside the VW, then began inching closer and closer. Jo threw a frantic look toward the impassive face of the driver of the other car. From his expression, she would never have guessed that he was slowly but surely trying to force her off the road.

Aware that the jolting of the two cars could harm her baby, Jo decided to let the rude, inconsiderate jerks have their way. She turned the wheel sharply to the right and felt the front tire scrape against the curb. "There," she muttered angrily, "the road's all yours." But instead of passing her as she'd hoped, the dark car angled directly in front of the VW.

Quick as lightning, both doors flew open and two men came rushing toward her. Jo was positively speechless when the door of the VW was opened, her arm grabbed by the taller of the two men. "Come with us," her assailant demanded in a brisk voice.

The paralysis holding her tongue in its grip vanished. Jo was furious. She locked her fingers around the steering wheel and regarded the man with haughty disdain. "You should be ashamed of yourself, running me off the road, then trying to force me from my car!"

"Just do as we say and you won't be hurt," the man assured her, his gaze riveted to Jo's protruding stomach. Suddenly he released his hold on her arm and turned to his companion. "They didn't say anything about her being pregnant!" he hissed.

The other man, stocky and ruddy-faced, stepped around so that he could get a better view of Jo. "Holy hell!" he exclaimed. "What are we supposed to do if she goes into labor?"

"You won't be called upon to do anything, you insufferable pig, because I'm not going with you," Jo said icily. The nerve of them! she fumed like a tiny volcano. Surely if she delayed them long enough, a police car would come by.

"I'm afraid we aren't asking you, lady, we're telling you."

"Which you can do till hell freezes over. I'm not moving an inch." If he would only look away, she was thinking frantically, she might have a chance of starting the car.

Before she could do anything to free herself, however, she felt her arm being grasped again. "I'm sorry, but you will have to come with us," the taller man said again. He reached over Jo and picked up her purse, handed it to his friend, then released the seat belt. "Will you please get out of the car?"

"No."

"If we have to force you, there is a strong possibility we might hurt your baby. Do you want that to happen?"

Jo favored him with a withering look, but realized what he said was true. A scuffle could harm the baby, and that was the last thing she wanted. She squirmed around in the seat until her feet hung over the bottom edge of the car. "Do you mind?" she asked regally, extending a hand to the man hovering over her.

"Of course not." He hoisted her to her feet, then carefully guided her to the waiting car.

"Er—when is your baby due?"

"Today," she replied nastily, getting the greatest of pleasures in seeing his face turn green.

The short, stocky man ran ahead and opened the back door, but his tall companion hesitated. "I'm not sure putting her in the backseat is a good idea, Stephano. She might get sick. The baby is due today."

The short man looked at Jo, horrified. "Are you sure?"

"Believe me, my condition is not a figment of my imagination," she said tartly. "I also get car sick when I travel in the backseat."

"Then it will have to be the front, Lars. We don't have time to stop every few miles. The plane leaves in an hour." Again Jo stood by while the men went into a hurried discussion. The more she listened, the more she was convinced she was being abducted by two weirdos, thrown completely off stride from fear of her having the baby while she was with them.

But as the gesturing became more involved, she caught a glimpse of a holstered pistol beneath the jacket of the stocky man called Stephano. Covert glances at Lars's waist revealed a similar suspi-

238

cious bump. Bungling weirdos might dress in nice suits as these men did, but holstered pistols? That struck Jo as cold, hard realism. They were professionals.

But why? Why her? Was she going to be held for ransom for some huge sum of money? Would anyone be able to help her? Could her father pay for her release? Her panic increased as she was forced into the passenger seat.

As the car swung onto the street at breakneck speed, Jo remembered some mention of a plane. They had said it would be leaving within the hour. She crossed her arms over her upper body, her hands clasping her elbows nervously. Where were they taking her? The brave show she'd put up thus far had begun to wane.

CHAPTER EIGHTEEN

Chase had no sooner entered his motel room when there was a knock at the door. He shrugged out of the light-tan jacket, jerked the tie from his neck, then reached for the ornate door handle.

"Who is it?" he asked before releasing the lock.

"Alex."

Chase opened the door and stepped back. "This is a switch. You weren't supposed to be here till tomorrow. I just left Garcia. He didn't mention you were in town yet. What's up?"

Alex, his brow furrowed, was silent for a moment. He walked over to the window and stared out, his hands braced on the wide window ledge. "There's been the damndest mix-up." He turned and faced Chase. "Lucy's still in Washington. She tripped getting out of a taxi last night and broke her ankle."

Chase shrugged. "In this business plans change, we both know that. I'll make some excuse at the desk about my wife being ill, and we'll go from there." He walked into the bathroom and began pouring scotch into two glasses. He added ice, a whisper of water, then moved over to where Alex was still standing. "Was Lucy's part in all this that important?"

"No." Alex shook his head as he accepted the drink and met Chase's curious gaze. "Not really, just extra precaution. But you haven't heard the rest. It appears as if our informant had an accomplice. I got a phone call from Dracus, the double agent I told you about. He wanted to know when we'd started using pregnant women in our operation."

"What the hell is that supposed to mean?"

"Someone alerted our enemies that we were sending Lucy to Houston. I'm afraid we were wrong in thinking we'd kept you a secret. They know you're here, why you're here, and that Lucy was to work with you."

"Good God, Alex!" Chase exclaimed. "You mean you actually asked a pregnant woman to take part in this kind of an operation?"

"No!" Alex threw up his hand. "And please don't cloud the issue, I'm just as confused as you are at this point. First of all, Lucy is not married and she is not pregnant. At least she wasn't three days ago when I had lunch with her in Washington. The best I could get from Dracus—and he was kind of rattled himself—is that two enemy agents began a surveillance of your home this morning. A brunette, driving a red VW, left your house. The two agents followed her, stopped the VW, and abducted her." He looked pleadingly at Chase. "Do you have any idea at all who this woman is?"

Chase felt his body turn ice cold with fear. For a moment Alex's face blurred before his eyes as what he'd just heard was absorbed. Jo. Jo had been kidnapped by enemy agents!

"You're damn right I know who the woman is," he answered in a low, harsh voice. "Her name's Jo Benoit, and she lives next door to me."

"Christ!" Alex paled. "This is terrible."

"Precisely!" Chase roared. "She's pregnant, and her baby is due in a week. Now I'd suggest you get Dracus back on that damn phone and make whatever arrangements are necessary to get her released."

"Well—I—I mean—"

"Don't give me all the organizational bullshit, Alex," Chase stormed, his face becoming an unhealthy shade of red. "I want Jo released, and I want it done now!"

"Hell, Chase, you know how these things work." Alex tried to inject reason into the conversation. "We're all caught up short by what's happened. I'm sure you're very fond of the woman, and we'll do everything possible to see that she's kept safe."

"Fond hell," Chase raged. "I love her! Love her,

do you hear me? I plan to marry her just as soon as the baby is born."

"Er—shouldn't it be the other way around?" a startled Alex asked. "I mean—did it take her being abducted to make you see where your duty lies?"

"Duty hell! The baby isn't mine, but it will be as soon as I can adopt it. So get cracking, Grenwyck, time's running out. Did Dracus give you any idea where they're holding Jo?"

"No," Alex said bleakly. "There is one thing you might get a kick out of though. It seems she's been giving her abductors hell. She told them her baby was due yesterday. Dracus said it was like a damned three-ring circus. They're afraid to take their eyes off her for fear she'll go into labor."

"That sounds like Jo," Chase said gruffly. He hit his palm with the tightly clenched fist of the other hand. "I feel so damned helpless. Just how far is this Dracus character willing to go to get her out of there?"

"That remains to be seen. About the only thing I can do at this point is make contact with Garcia. He's more familiar with the setup down here than we are. If he can't get results, then I'll get in touch with Washington. I hate to mention this, but there *is* the microfilm to think of."

"I don't give a royal damn about the microfilm!" Chase shouted. "All I'm interested in is seeing the woman I love walk through that door."

"Look"—Alex shook his head—"you know I'll

do everything I can. You do know that, don't you?"

"I know," Chase replied tersely. He swung around and strode to the window. Jo's life was in danger because of him, and there wasn't a damn thing he could do about it. He thought of the times they'd been together, of the times he'd held her in his arms. He could almost feel her silken skin beneath his fingertips. He closed his eyes, the taste of her lips coming readily to mind. He could hear her voice, late in the evenings when he'd bully her into walking with him. He saw her face as she practiced the breathing exercises in the natural childbirth classes, saw her teasing him as he coached her. Now she was with strangers, frightened and alone. Not knowing from one minute to the next if she would live or die.

Jo opened her eyes, surprised to find that she'd dozed off. She brought her wrist close to her face, but even then, she couldn't make out the time. All she knew was that she was in Mexico City. It had been dark when she dropped off to sleep, and it still was. She turned onto her side, the slight movement bringing the shadowy outline of one of her abductors to the doorway of the bedroom. "Are you all right?" the one called Lars asked politely, but coolly.

"I'm miserable," Jo said bluntly, and meant it. Her back hurt, her head hurt, and she felt lousy in

244

general. She was frightened, locked in a hotel suite with two total strangers, and she was fast approaching a nervous breakdown.

"Are you in pain?" he asked, hoping against hope that she would say no.

Jo was about to give her usual reply, when a thought came to her. Perhaps she would be able to escape if she could convince her two captors that her labor had started.

"I'm not sure," she hedged, her mind whirling with indecision. "I have a terrible backache and the most peculiar pains in my stomach." She raised herself up on one elbow. "Do either of you know anything about delivering a baby?"

She saw Lars stiffen. He stood as though paralyzed, then quickly turned and disappeared. Moments later Jo could hear the heated discussion taking place between him and Stephano. She sank back onto the bed, her body tense as she waited.

Before their argument was settled, however, they were interrupted by a knock on the door. Jo strained to hear who the visitor was. But the only sound she could make out was a resumption of the former conversation, now helped along by a third deeper voice, heavily accented.

Suddenly the newest addition to the group could be heard distinctly. "You took the wrong woman, I tell you!"

An excited babble arose as Lars and Stephano defended themselves, then the conversation became very hushed, and Jo could feel her body trembling.

"It'll cost you. Disposing of a pregnant woman is not a very pleasant thing." It was the voice of the visitor. Jo jammed a hand against her lips to keep from screaming. "The best thing the two of you can do is get out of the country. I'll call Brussels and explain, then I'll dispose of the woman."

The voices of the men became hushed and garbled. Jo thought she heard the word microfilm, but she couldn't be sure. Her heart was beating so loud, it sounded like a drum about to leap from her chest.

"Don't worry, the microfilm is already on its way. You should know that was taken care of first. But this woman has made the situation messy. I'm afraid this little incident won't look too good on your records. I'd suggest you take a walk while I try to clean up this mess you've made."

Apparently Lars and Stephano believed the man, because Jo could hear movement in the room and then the sound of a door closing. She remained perfectly still, her body as rigid as a board. Some sixth sense warned her she wasn't alone in the suite, though for the life of her, she couldn't detect the slightest noise.

She was never quite certain how long she waited. But it dawned on her that when one's life was hanging on a thread, time passed with incredible swiftness. When the shadowy figure of a short, broad man filled the doorway, Jo knew her moment had come. He was going to kill her.

Rather than the panic she was certain would fill her body and mind when the end came, Jo was surprised to find herself coldly calm. Some inner strength kept her from crying out, from begging for her life. She watched the man cross the room, her eyes never wavering as he came to a halt beside the bed.

He bent over her, his face coming so close to hers, she could feel his breath on her cheek. Jo stiffened, then closed her eyes, waiting for the feel of his hands on her throat . . .

"Mrs. Benoit," the man whispered close to her ear. "Can you hear me?"

Yes, Jo wanted to scream out, but she didn't.

"I'm not going to hurt you, but you must cooperate with me," he told her. "The room is probably bugged, so don't speak above a whisper. Do you understand?"

Jo wavered with indecision. But if she had to die, she knew she would rather be on her feet than lying defenseless on her back. "I understand," she replied, and opened her eyes. She could barely make out the man's forehead, heavy brows, and large nose. His hair appeared thick and dark, and his shoulders were massive. "Who are you?" she murmured in a barely audible whisper.

"My name doesn't matter," he said, his lips

hardly moving. "The important thing is to get you out of here. Can you walk?"

"Yes, but I need my shoes. I think they put them over there, along with my purse," she told him, pointing toward the double closet on the other side of the room.

Her mysterious benefactor moved with the swiftness of a cat, and within seconds he was back. He dropped the shoes and purse on the bed, then caught Jo by her upper arms and pulled her into a sitting position. She saw him kneel, then felt his hands on her ankle and the cool leather of her shoes as they were slipped onto her feet.

"Come." He caught her hand and pulled her to her feet. "We have very little time."

Jo followed him—she had no other choice. As they rushed through the sitting room of the suite, she saw his face, and in that brief moment she knew she would never forget it. His eyes were dark, almost black. They met hers for a shattering second, and Jo was stricken by the lack of emotion she saw mirrored there.

The next few minutes were a blur as they rushed the length of a long corridor, then plunged down two flights of stairs, the man's muscled arm holding her close to his side, his powerful body practically carrying her.

At the bottom of the stairs, he placed Jo against the wall, then reached out cautiously to open a door a few inches. She watched while he apparently satisfied himself of their escape route. He reached for her again. They stepped through the door into an alley that was pitch black, but the lack of light didn't seem to faze the man. He rushed her forward with the same speed with which they'd left the suite.

Suddenly, toward the end of the alley, the outline of a car became distinguishable. Jo found herself being placed into the front seat from the driver's side, the man following close behind her. "All right so far?" He threw her a brief glance as he started the engine and began to edge the car forward.

"Fine," she answered faintly. "But will you please tell me where we're going? I heard you back there, you know. I heard you telling Lars and Stephano you would dispose of me."

She saw a flash of white teeth and heard a harsh, bitter chuckle. "Would you rather I took you back?" he taunted her.

"No—no, I suppose not," Jo stammered.

"Don't worry. Soon you will be with friends. Maybe you won't think so badly of me then, mmm?"

Jo didn't have an answer.

Her head became dizzy as the car sped down one street after another, turning the corners on two wheels, and taking advantage of the shortcuts through other dimly lit, cluttered alleys. Once Jo had to press her knuckles against her lips to keep from screaming out when she saw the figure of a man jump aside, the edge of the front fender brushing against his arm.

From the alley Jo saw that they were entering another street. But they'd gone only a short distance when the brakes were suddenly applied and a hard turn on the wheel sent them down a sharp incline into an underground parking garage. The car came to an abrupt stop. The door on Jo's side was flung open, and she found herself looking straight into Chase's eyes.

CHAPTER NINETEEN

The lights in the airplane flashed on, telling the passengers to fasten their seat belts. The voice of the captain came over the intercom to inform them that they would be landing in Houston within minutes. The sound of his voice droned on, but Jo wasn't listening. The anger consuming her had left her blind, deaf, and dumb!

"You will have to talk to me eventually," a harassed Chase muttered as he leaned across her to fasten the seat belt. Instead of moving back, he remained poised over her, one long arm braced on the left arm of her seat. "You were never supposed to become involved. Why won't you believe me?"

Jo stared straight ahead, the nervous quivering of her body beginning to lessen slightly only in the last few minutes. She'd lived through a nightmare, an absolute nightmare. Worse still, she told herself, there was a double-dealing, obnoxious jackass seated beside her, constantly entreating her to forgive him. Never, she vowed maliciously, never!

"I called Elise. She's going to be waiting for you at home. Was that all right?"

Jo remained silent.

"She said she would have your brothers and your mother come over as well. Maybe even your father, if he can get away for a few minutes," Chase said innocently, then leaned back and waited for the explosion.

"You didn't!" Jo said furiously, her gray eyes shooting darts of anger at him. "How dare you interfere in my personal life after what you've done? And why are you grinning?" she demanded.

"Because you're talking to me," Chase pointed out. "When we get married, I do hope you won't continue these bouts of pouting, sweetheart," he said softly. "I believe you told me once that it causes digestive problems."

"Go to hell!" Jo spluttered. She tried to turn her back to him, but the seat belt wouldn't budge. "I really think I hate you."

"No, princess, you don't hate me. You love me." He smiled confidently.

"I've changed my mind."

"Not so." Chase shook his head. "When you were asleep a while ago, and your head was resting on my arm, I distinctly heard you say you loved me."

"A person can't be held responsible for what she says in her sleep." She tried to inch away from the arm that had materialized across her shoulders, but it followed like a shadow.

252

"Too bad. Marrying a man you hate doesn't make any sense."

"I am not going to marry you, you—you gangster!"

"I also plan on adopting the baby. However, I do wish you would decide on a girl's name. I don't like the idea of my daughter going through the first few days of her life without a name."

"You will not adopt my baby! I will raise my child by myself, and I will thank you not to worry about a name."

Suddenly a head appeared between them from the seats behind. Jo and Chase looked around, startled. "Marry him, my child," a kindly voice urged Jo. It was an elderly priest, the authority of his collar visible beneath his chin. "The child of unwed parents has a heavy cross to bear in this world. This young man really does seem to care for you, you know."

Jo glared at the intruder. "Go sit on a tack!" Chase smothered his laughter, and the priest patted him on the shoulder.

"God bless you, son, you have a heavy cross to bear as well."

"How can you be so rude to a man of the cloth?" Chase whispered tauntingly in Jo's ear. "The poor man was only looking out for the baby."

"Would you like me to tell him that you are a G-man? That without any thought or consideration for anyone, you will fly off to any godfor-saken spot on the globe at a moment's notice and do who-knows-what to some poor unsuspecting person?"

"But I'm no longer a—er—G-man," Chase calmly told her. "My cover has been blown. I'm useless for that type of work now."

Jo felt herself weakening, and she worked hard to maintain her present level of annoyance. "I'm sure you'll think of something just as interesting to pass the time."

"Oh, I have." He leaned close, his lips brushing the sensitive tip of her ear. "I plan to devote all my time and energy making love to you. How does that sound?"

"I've had better offers," she said lightly.

Chase's hand tightened around her fingers to a bone-crushing grip. "Then I suggest you forget about them," he said harshly. "I'm damn well your present, and I'll definitely be your future."

"If I decide to let you be." Jo turned and met his jealous gaze. "As a future, you're not very reliable. I can't offer you the kind of excitement you seem to crave, nor do I have any intention of picking up and traipsing off to some dust bowl in order for you to get your kicks out of life. I'm a creature of habit, as are most females. I dislike changes in my life."

"You sound like a narrowminded little mule."

"That may well be, but it's my way. I don't want

your friend Alex or Dracus popping in and out of my life. They make me nervous."

"You seemed to like Alex well enough back there at the airport," Chase retorted, scowling. "You stuck by him like a leech," he accused, remembering the hot surge of jealousy that shot through him as he watched.

"There was no one else for me to stick to." She looked away.

"I was there."

"So you were."

"Dracus saved your life. Have you forgotten that?"

"I have not, and I thanked him. But that doesn't mean I want him to share my future." She looked thoughtful for a moment, then turned back to Chase. "Didn't you tell me he was a double agent?"

Chase shrugged. "He is. And someday he'll play the odds the wrong way and he'll be killed."

"You don't like him?"

"I would have liked the devil if he'd brought you back to me, Jo. But to answer your question, no, I've never thought much of double agents. They're only out for highest price. Men like Dracus are born without a conscience. If you're in the same business, you learn to accept them. Even they have their uses."

"Like what he did back there in Mexico City?" Jo asked softly.

"Exactly. He even managed to get the microfilm to Alex."

"Do you think they'll catch him?"

"Who knows? Try to put Dracus and all that happened this weekend out of your mind. The espionage business is a dirty but necessary part of our society."

"The enemy agents who abducted me," Jo began. "They weren't indifferent to my condition. In fact, they were almost kind."

"Why not? They had time on their hands. They were holding you to stop us from trying to get the microfilm back. Once they became aware of their mistake, they were willing to hand you over to Dracus."

Jo shuddered, unconsciously inching closer against the comforting warmth of Chase. "How can I forget? I was listening in the next room."

That sobering comment brought the conversation to a halt. In the few minutes it took for the plane to land, Chase stared thoughtfully into space, one arm around Jo, his other hand rubbing at his chin. Not only had his cover been blown, but he'd been forced to stand by and depend on a man for whom he had nothing but contempt to save the woman he loved. He tried to think of his life without Jo in it, but the bleakness of such a future chilled him to the bone.

Jo moved restlessly, the low pains in her back intensifying as each new one came on. She stretched out her legs, in hopes of arching her body and finding some relief. The pain went away, and she relaxed. But in seconds the pain was back. Only this time it seemed to grab her from her waist to her thighs, with an acuteness that brought a startled gasp from her lips.

Chase's arm around her shoulder tightened. His free hand came to rest on her stomach. "What's wrong?" he muttered hoarsely just as the first jarring impact of the plane touching down jolted the passengers.

Jo turned an anxious face to him, her lips drawn tight against her teeth. "I think I'm in labor," she managed to whisper.

As frantic as her flight from the hotel in Mexico City had been, her removal from the plane by the paramedics and her ride to the hospital were even more harrowing. This time there were no alleys to cut through, only the sound of the siren, and Chase's gentle voice urging her to remember what her instructor had said and relax.

The last thing Jo remembered was telling Chase that she was relaxed. She smiled at him, then promptly passed out. She regained consciousness long enough to focus her gaze on Chase, who looked like death. A slight movement of her hand brought him to her side.

"You look terrible," she whispered, bringing his hand to her lips and pressing them against his palm. "How can you be my coach if you don't shape up?" she teased drowsily.

"I love you, sweetheart," Chase whispered, his eyes revealing the torment he was going through.

A movement over his shoulder made Jo look up. Her mother? she smiled dreamily. What was her mother doing there? Where was Elise? She really wanted Elise.

"I'm right here, Jo," her sister's voice came from the other side of the gurney, and a cool hand rested against her cheek.

Jo sighed contentedly, then closed her eyes, and slipped into unconsciousness.

A smartly dressed Jo stepped briskly from the VW and hurried into the house. A worried look was the only jarring note about her entire person as she entered the kitchen. She'd promised Elise she'd be back by four o'clock, and it was now five-thirty. Jo sighed, stopping long enough to put down the bag of groceries she was carrying. Doctors, shopping, and babies! Those three categories probably accounted for more than half the nervous breakdowns in the world.

She stopped and listened. Hearing nothing, she gave a quick prayer of thankfulness, then tiptoed on down the hall. The sight that greeted her when she entered the nursery brought her to a standstill.

Chase and Elise were each sitting in matching

rocking chairs, each holding a smiling, gurgling baby.

"Now I know why my children are spoiled!" She tried to sound stern. "Every time either of you babysit, they cry for hours after you leave."

"Babies should be held. It gives them confidence," Elise spouted like an expert.

"And you?" Jo turned to Chase, who barely acknowledged her presence, he was so busy making the most peculiar noises to "his" baby. "What's your excuse?"

"I happen to like babies." He smiled lazily at her. "Sue me." He promptly dismissed her, returning to his former job of entertaining the tiny bundle he held in his arms.

"You're both disgusting," Jo said with a sigh. She went back to the kitchen, returning with two boxes of diapers, which she opened and rearranged in the diaper holders hanging on the end of each crib.

"What did Marie have to say?" Chase asked, his sharp gaze running over the enticing lines of her body, made even more attractive by the one-piece red knit dress.

"I'm healthy as a horse and I still have a few pounds of extra weight on me," she answered, then picked up the empty diaper boxes. "That means I have to go on a diet."

"Forget the diet," Chase told her. He rose to his feet and walked over to the bed with the pink fuzzy blanket. Jo watched him place the sleeping baby on her tummy, his large hand gently stroking the child as he soothed her back to sleep. When he was convinced all was well with the baby, he straightened, then turned to Jo.

"You look lovely. Have dinner with me this evening." His voice was like a caress, and Jo felt herself grow warm beneath his gaze.

"I—I can't," she stammered, the panic building up inside her, making a rosy glow creep over her cheeks.

"I'll be glad to volunteer for babysitting duty." Elise spoke up, her presence forgotten by Jo in the maelstrom of feeling created by Chase. "Mary Clare will be glad to help me, if that will make you feel better."

"You spend too much of your time over here as it is," Jo wavered, torn between wanting to be with Chase and not imposing on her sister. Elise had been like a rock since the twins were born, but she needed to get out as well.

"Alex will probably drop by later," Chase added, and Jo caught the interested sparkle in her sister's eye.

"All right," she gave in. "But we'll have to be home early. I like to feed them their bedtime bottle myself." She smiled, her eyes touching on the pink bundle Chase had placed in one crib and the sleeping face of her tiny son Elise was still holding.

"I'll have you home by nine-thirty," Chase

agreed, "but not a minute sooner. It isn't healthy the way you hover over these two."

"I don't hover," Jo protested, though in her own mind she had to admit she hardly ever left the twins.

"If you two will excuse me, I'll think I'll put Ian to bed." Elise thought it best to interrupt the difference of opinion before it turned into a full-scale battle. After tucking the blanket around the sleeping baby, she looked brightly from Chase to Jo. "Do I have time to run over to my place and get some work I brought home from the office?"

The restaurant Chase had chosen was tucked in an out-of-the-way place, the prices exorbitant, and the food delicious. Jo glanced around her as they were shown to their table. Lance had brought her to this same place several times.

She settled back in the comfortable chair, her gaze on Chase as he gave the waiter their order for drinks. He was dressed in another impeccably tailored dark suit, and she had never seen him looking better. He even looked rested, something she couldn't understand, considering the long hours he put in at the office and the time he spent with her. The lines of fatigue on his face she'd noticed during their Mexico fiasco and while she was in the hospital had disappeared. In fact, he looked better now than at anytime since she'd known him.

"Is there a spot on my nose?" Chase asked after

sitting still under her careful scrutiny for several minutes.

Jo blushed, praying the soft glow of candlelight would hide the heightened color in her cheeks. "I'm sorry, I didn't mean to stare."

"I'm not complaining." Chase smiled lazily. "Being stared at by a beautiful woman is a pleasure anytime."

"Your ego is showing, Mr. Colbern," Jo teased him.

"I can't be perfect all the time, Ms. Benoit. Especially when you're wearing a dress with a neckline that low," he drawled innocently.

"If you weren't such a pervert, you'd have no reason to be bothered by my neckline." She smiled sweetly, unable to stop her hand from hovering over that part of her anatomy that was holding his undivided attention.

"A dead man would be bothered by that dress, honey. If that makes me a pervert, then so be it."

The waiter brought their drinks, left menus, then faded into the dimness.

Jo tried to appear unaffected by the exchange of words, but nothing on earth short of a steel wall could protect her from the glowing intensity of Chase's eyes as they went about seducing her across the table.

"How are things at the office?" she asked after taking a sip of her drink.

"Things are fine. I'm adjusting well, and I haven't the slightest desire to wander."

"Oh. That's nice. I'm sure your father is pleased."

"I really couldn't say," Chase replied easily. "I wasn't thinking of his peace of mind when I made the decision."

"Oh."

"Is that all you have to say? Just 'Oh'?"

"No—I mean—I think it's great." Jo swallowed nervously, then gulped down a huge amount of her drink.

"I'd go light with that if I were you," Chase warned. "Your ability to hold your liquor leaves a great deal to be desired."

"Are you afraid I'll drink too much and embarrass you?" Jo grinned.

"No way, sweetheart. Nothing you could do would ever embarrass me." He leaned forward and caught her hand that was fingering the rim of the glass. His clasp was warm and strong, and Jo was powerless to control the electric charge that surged through her at his touch. It was no surprise, it happened each time he put his hands on her. Whether he was helping her from the car, holding her elbow as they walked, or simply placing his hand against her back when she went before him, Chase's slightest touch left her feeling breathless, throwing her center of gravity out of sync.

"I couldn't do anything to embarrass you?" she said teasingly. "What about the Club Eros?"

"I said embarrass, not infuriate." Chase tipped his head and grinned. "I'm afraid I overreacted to that little escapade, but you scared the hell out of me. You could have been hurt in a crowd like that. You and the babies."

"I'm sorry," Jo said softly. "It was never my intention to worry you." She looked at their clasped hands, then back at Chase. "Was that why you went dashing off to Mexico without telling me good-bye?" It was something that had been gnawing at her for weeks now.

"In a way, I suppose it was. That and the lecture Jake gave me."

"Jake? Why would he lecture you?"

"Jake is always lecturing me," Chase chuckled. "It's his way of whipping me into shape. As to why, it involved you."

"And?" Jo prodded.

"He suggested, in his uniquely blunt fashion, that I was making a royal ass of myself where you were concerned. He said I was making your life miserable by hovering over you. Alex called about that time, we had lunch, he asked my help and I decided to go."

"Just like that?" Jo asked disbelievingly. "Couldn't you have waited and explained?"

"I was angry at you, at Jake, and at myself. Getting away for a few days seemed the perfect solu-

264

tion for everyone. Though it sure as hell didn't turn out that way."

"Please." Jo closed her eyes for a moment. "When I think of you having done that sort of thing for years and years, I want to clobber you. Didn't you ever think of Bink? Of your parents? Were you *trying* to get yourself killed?"

"Nothing so dramatic, I assure you." Chase shrugged. "Bink's mother and I were having problems even before he was born. She wanted a husband who would come home every evening and spend each weekend with her at the country club. That wasn't my way."

"Then why get married in the first place?"

"The story isn't very original, I'm afraid," Chase frowned. "I'd just returned from an eight-month stint in the Middle East. There was a party and I went. Marge was there, beautiful, exciting, and looking for a husband. Our courtship lasted all of six weeks. Before the honeymoon was over we both realized the mistake. In a few months Bink was on the way, and I headed for Venezuela. When she died three years later, I hired Jake, brought Bink to Houston, and life went on as usual."

"At least you're honest about it." Jo stared into the amber liquid of her drink.

"There's no reason not to be. Marge was a fine person. She would have been the perfect wife for a young executive, and she was a hell of a good mother. I just didn't love her enough to want to be with her the rest of my life." Chase watched the play of emotions on Jo's face, his shrewd gaze missing nothing. "I think it's time we ordered, don't you?" he asked casually.

Jo nodded, her thoughts in a turmoil. Honest he had been, she thought sadly, so honest, in fact, the words he'd spoken cut through her dreams like the cold, hard edge of a knife. Chase Colbern was like a magnificent bird of prey, his freedom as necessary to his existence as the air he breathed.

Dinner was delicious, as Jo had known it would be. But for all the attention she gave the food on her plate, it could very well have been straw. Chase did most of the talking, and Jo responded. She smiled at all the appropriate moments, asked the right questions, and even managed to laugh at his dry humor. After all, she kept telling herself, this is the man I love.

True to his word, Chase kept a close watch on the time. At nine-fifteen, they were on their way home. When they reached Jo's house, she turned to say good night, wanting to be alone with her thoughts.

"I've upset you, haven't I?" Chase asked, ignoring the haunted look in her eyes and pulling her into his arms.

"What makes you say that?" She tried to sound unconcerned.

"Because I know what you're thinking," he replied soberly. "We happen to love each other, sweetheart. And no amount of pretending on your part can hide that look I see in your eyes. I don't like to see you unhappy. I worry about you. I worry about the twins. I love them, just as I love you. Can't you see that?"

"Oh, yes," Jo whispered, unable to resist touching her lips to his. But instead of allowing the kiss to deepen, as was Chase's intention, she drew back. "I see the love in your eyes, I feel it in your touch, Chase. But is it enough to hold you? Will you wake up one morning and decide you're bored?"

"No."

"You say it so easily. And your relationship with Alex. You thought that was finished once before also, didn't you? But it wasn't, was it?"

Chase ignored the questions. The feel of her breasts pressed against his chest had created an aching need for her that was slowly driving him out of his mind. His lips descended on hers, his tongue thrusting into the heat of her waiting mouth. His hands ran feverishly over her body, one hand finding its way inside the inviting neckline of the dress, to the creamy mound of her breast and the rigid thrust of the nipple waiting for his touch.

The soft, purring sounds that came from Jo and Chase's heavy breathing were the only sounds inside the car. Jo felt the waves of desire washing over her, felt the pull of the emotional tide destroying her defenses against this man. She wanted him,

267

wanted to feel the touch of his hands not only on her breasts, but over every inch of her body. She wanted to be able to see him, wanted to feel his skin against her skin.

Her fingers inched their way to the buttons of his shirt. In seconds the way was clear to her, her unerring fingertips darting like quicksilver through the thick, wiry hair covering his chest. She found the flat, rigid male nipples and teased them, glorying in the feel of power when she heard the harsh groan in the back of Chase's throat.

She felt the tremors hit his powerful body, then knew a moment of disappointment when his lips left her mouth and touched the throbbing pulse in her throat.

"Marry me, Jo," he murmured in a voice as overwrought with passion as she knew her own must be. "I can't keep on touching you, holding you in my arms and not make love to you. I've become a walking zombie."

"You make it sound so simple," she whispered in a trembling voice, her head resting on his chest, the rapid beating of his heart beneath her ear.

"Then say yes, damn it," Chase demanded, his arms tightening till Jo was sure her ribs would break. "I need you. I need you with me all the time, not just a few minutes in the evening or during the day."

"I need time, Chase, and so do you."

"For what?" he said with a growl. "You know I want you. You have to know."

And Jo did. She could feel the thrust of his arousal against her thigh and see the thin sheen of perspiration on his forehead. "I want time enough for you to know me when I'm not dependent on you. I want to show you that I can function as a person without you constantly looking over my shoulder. You've carried me, emotionally and in many other ways, from the day I found out I was pregnant. And daffy though you think I am, it's important to me as an individual to regain my independence."

"Are you trying to say you won't marry me?" Chase asked in a quiet voice.

"No. I want to marry you. But I want to come to you as an equal, not as a clinging woman, afraid to face life. I also want you to be sure."

"I happen to be short on patience where you're concerned," he warned her. "And I won't stop trying to get you in my bed."

"Good." Jo smiled. "I can't think of a nicer problem than being chased by you. Court me, Chase, send me flowers, but allow me this time to find myself again."

"You're making sense, and I don't like it," he said, scowling.

"I know." Jo smiled tenderly, her lips grazing his stubborn jaw. "You'd much prefer me as the screwy dame looking to you for help, wouldn't you?"

"Yes."

"Then don't panic. There is more than one side to my personality, Chase. Sit back and watch the real me unfold."

CHAPTER TWENTY

Elise swept into the kitchen just as Jo was sitting down to feed Ian his breakfast. Her sister looked radiant, the deep-rose suit bringing out the color in her cheeks and playing up her beautiful dark hair. Their relationship was growing deeper each day, and Jo was delighted. They argued, they teased each other, and they didn't worry about hurt feelings. Each had accepted the other, and the feeling between them was sound and good.

"Why do you always feed that little squirt before Lisy?" Elise demanded in mock sternness. She bent over her tiny, fist-waving nephew and chucked him under his two chins, her face beaming with love.

"Because your niece is much more cooperative about such matters," Jo remarked dryly as she eased a spoonful of mashed carrots into her son's tiny mouth. "And I do wish you wouldn't call her Lisy. When I named her after you, I just knew you would turn the lovely name of Kathryn Elise into Lisy."

271

Elise blithely ignored her sister's early-morning grouchiness. She removed the jacket of her expensive suit, donned one of the cover-up aprons, then picked up her niece from the Port-a-Crib. "Don't worry, Lisy." She smiled sweetly at Jo, then looked back at the baby. "Aunt Elise is here to make sure you aren't neglected."

"In a pig's eye!" Jo softly exclaimed, though she had to smile as she watched Elise handle the awkward manipulations of baby, cereal, and the continuous wipe-up that accompanied each of the twins' meals. "I must say, you do that quite well."

"I've found that I like babies," Elise murmured, her lips pursed humorously as she spooned food into Lisy's waiting mouth. "I think I'll have two or three myself."

"Get married first," Jo advised her. "It's got to be easier with a husband to help you. I think," she tacked on.

"If that's the case, then why haven't you married Chase?"

"I have my reasons," Jo said quietly.

"What was his reaction when you told him you were going out of town on business? It is the second time in three weeks."

"He . . . wasn't thrilled, to say the least. But I feel I have to do it." Jo sighed. "Mary Clare has shouldered way more than her share of the load for months now. She needs some time to be with Mo."

272

"I'm sure that pleases you."

"It does. I've done everything imaginable to get those two together, and now that they are actually seeing each other without fighting, I feel rather proud of myself." She threw Elise a considering glance. "Now I have to start working on another project."

"Your mother is a busybody," Elise muttered to the baby she was feeding, her face suffused with color.

"True"—Jo chuckled—"but you and Alex do seem to have so much in common, I can't resist."

"Then force yourself," she was bluntly told. "I'm quite capable of looking after my own life. If I decide I want Alex Grenwyck, then you can rest assured I'll get him."

"Hear that, Ian?" Jo told her son. "Your Aunt Elise is bringing home a new uncle for you. What do you think about that?"

After the twins had been fed, bathed, and put down for their morning nap, Elise rushed off to the office. Jo straightened up the house, then settled down to get some work done in her studio.

As she worked, she found herself thinking over the last few weeks and her relationship with Chase. He had reluctantly accepted her decision to wait, though Jo had to smile as she thought of the inexhaustible excuses he found for dropping in. She knew he loved the twins, just as she loved Bink, and that was the way she wanted it. She'd gotten to know his family better, and they appeared to have accepted her without the slightest reservation. She and the twins had gone with Bink and Chase over to the Colberns' twice, and Sybil and Matthew had welcomed her and her babies into their home and their hearts.

And yet Jo still found herself holding back. Instead of seeing Chase every night, as she had while she was pregnant, she pretended to be busy, wanting to let their time together be special. And it was. Chase took her to dinner, he took her dancing, and twice they had attended a local dinner theater. They were seeing each other in different roles, and Jo hoped it was the right thing to do. It had to be, she told herself. She didn't want to lose Chase, but the time she'd begged for had been as much for him as for herself.

The day passed quickly, and by the middle of the afternoon she had managed to complete the series of designs she would be taking with her on the three-day trip. Jo hurried to take a shower and dress by four o'clock. Amelia Tavers was due to arrive at that time, and Jo wanted everything to go smoothly.

Of the four women she had interviewed as housekeeper-nanny for the children, Amelia had been her favorite. The plump, matronly woman wasn't the best dressed of the four, nor the most intellectual one of the group. She was a widow, alone, and needed to work. There was also a warmth about her and a commonsense attitude that made Jo know the twins would be safe with her.

By the time Chase arrived at seven to take her out to dinner, Jo felt as though she'd been on a merry-go-round most of the day.

Chase looked over at her and smiled when he heard the small sigh rush past her lips as she relaxed against the seat of the car and closed her eyes.

"Busy day?"

"And how!" Jo turned her head and grinned at him. "What with leaving day after tomorrow, I tried to get everything done today. How about you?"

"I'm beginning to see why my father was so anxious for me to take over the firm so that he could retire." Chase chuckled. "I'm surprised he hasn't had a heart attack."

"Are you liking it any better?" Jo asked curiously.

"Surprisingly, I am. I'd never really been involved in the business from the planning stage before. It's interesting, and time consuming." He shot her a knowing glance. "Still worried that I'll pick up and steal away some dark night?"

Jo stuck out her tongue at him. "How well you know me. I'm not sure I like that."

"Then you'd better get used to it," Chase told her. He caught her hand and carried it to rest on his thigh. "I plan to stick so close to you, sweetheart, you will think you've grown an extra head."

"The twins should like that," she quipped, then wondered why he hadn't said anything about her trip. At first he'd been violently against her leaving the babies. Now he was accepting it without comment.

Throughout the evening, Jo waited. She baited the trap by mentioning her travel plans, the hotel where she would be staying in Dallas, and made several other pointed references to the fact that she would be away for three days. Chase listened, gave his advice on a couple of questions, but not a word did he utter regarding his disapproval of her decision to go.

When they were home, Chase stole in to see the twins and talk with Amelia for a few minutes. Then he further surprised her by announcing he was going out of town the next morning.

"When did this come up?" Jo asked suspiciously. She was standing in the circle of his arms, her hands resting on his shoulders.

"This morning," he said softly. "I have to go to Washington on business—business for the firm," he added and grinned. "I give you my word I'm not off on some nefarious plot with Alex. Besides, Elise has him going in circles. He keeps telling me what a wonderful place Houston is. I wonder if it would be as interesting if your sister weren't here."

"I don't know about that." Jo frowned. "I'm more concerned with when you're coming back."

Something flickered in Chase's eyes, a sudden light that Jo's sudden rush of misery failed to see. "Two, three days. We'll probably get back around the same time. Why? Was there something you wanted me to do for you?" he asked innocently.

"No." She shook her head. "I was just curious, that's all. Will I see you in the morning before you leave?"

"I doubt it, honey. My plane leaves at five-thirty A.M. You'll still be sleeping."

"I wish you'd told me sooner," Jo added petulantly.

Chase dipped his head, his mouth taking possession of hers with a suddenness that left Jo breathless. Her hands on his shoulders dug into the fabric of his jacket for support, her knees becoming weak. Chase drew back enough to look into her eyes, his breathing harsh and erratic. "Take care of yourself, princess, while I'm gone."

Jo nodded mutely, her hands trailing down his arms as they slowly released her. "You too," she whispered, feeling cut adrift as she watched him walk to the door, turn and look at her for a moment, then leave.

She remained staring at the closed door, while in her mind she was calling herself all sorts of idiot names. Chase was going away for days and hadn't mentioned it till the last minute. She didn't like it —didn't like it one little bit.

Jo unlocked the door of her hotel room and went in, kicking off her taupe-color high heels the moment she locked the door behind her. Lord, but she was tired. She'd met with two different groups during the day. One had signed a contract to carry Personal Touch Greeting Cards on the spot. The other had needed to confer with one other person. Jo was to have their decision the next day.

A brief glance at her watch showed that it was almost six o'clock. She shrugged out of her tweed jacket and skirt and was unbuttoning the blouse, when there was a knock at the door. She frowned. She had friends in Dallas, but thinking her time would be limited, she hadn't called to make plans to see anyone.

"Who is it?" Jo asked, her fingers quickly rebuttoning the blouse.

"Bellboy, Mrs. Benoit," the muffled voice replied. "The desk forgot to put a message in your box."

"Oh—just a minute." Jo fumbled with the chain, then opened the door a few inches and poked her head around the corner, straight into a huge bouquet of red roses. Behind the roses stood Chase.

"You're supposed to be in Washington," Jo said

stupidly, her heart beginning to race like crazy at the sight of him.

"I got lonesome. May I come in?"

"Yes." She stood, her hands reaching out for the flowers. "These are beautiful. I hope they are for me." She smiled, feeling shy and unsure of herself for some strange reason.

Chase closed the door with the tip of his shoe and then simply stood and stared at Jo.

She looked up from where her nose was buried amid the crimson buds, her breath catching in her throat. There was a look in Chase's eyes that sent the blood rushing through her veins like rivers of molten lava. The message she saw there was as real as the scent of the flowers wafting around her. And whether or not she was aware of it, her answer was just as clearly given.

"Put the roses down, Jo," he said softly, the timbre of his voice sending tiny shivers over her skin. She set the flowers on the edge of the dresser and turned back to face him. She saw his arms open and saw him take a step toward her. Without thinking, Jo found herself in his arms, unaware of having moved at all.

"God! I've missed you so much," Chase murmured as his lips rained quick, fevered kisses on her face, her eyes, her lips, and her throat. His hands were like fire, slipping beneath the edge of her blouse and burning their way over the smooth surface of her back and shoulders.

279

Jo felt the warmth of his nearness stealing over her. She gritted her teeth against the tiny explosions of pleasure rippling throughout her entire being. Chase was here, she was in his arms, and nothing else mattered.

"I hope you weren't planning on going out, because I'm going to make love to you." His voice was raspy. He caught her face between his hands, his lips nibbled at her mouth before plunging in and setting loose another super-charged rush of desire.

"I just got in," Jo whispered.

Chase caught her up in his arms and strode to the bed, then eased her to the floor, his arms keeping her locked against his body, his gaze never leaving her face. "I may be rushing you, I don't know. But if I don't make love to you right now, I think I will die. Can you understand that?"

"More than you know," Jo said simply. She reached up and pushed the dark suit jacket from his shoulders, then began pulling at the knot of his tie.

Large tanned hands became busy with according her the same treatment, and in moments the last bit of clothing fell in a forgotten heap at their feet.

Chase placed his hands on her hips, his eyes running possessively over her naked body. "You are so beautiful to me," he said slowly. "I've dreamed of this moment for so long."

Jo felt the same weakening sensation attacking her limbs she always felt when Chase touched her. Her body began to tremble, and his hold at her waist tightened. She caught at his arms for support, seeing the light of understanding in his eyes. But instead of resenting the power he held over her, Jo felt passion. She scanned the bold, massive lines of his body, the artist in her seeing balance and depth and the overall perfection that molded each part of him into a warm, breathing being. In that brief moment of scrutiny, she saw the proof of his manhood, as bold and proud as the man himself. Her hand reached out and touched him. She felt the quiver run through his body, saw him throw back his head as her fingers caressed him.

The slightest push from Chase sent them sprawling to the bed, his large body coming down beside hers, his hands fitting themselves to her hips and her breasts with unerring accuracy. Before Jo could draw a shattered breath, she felt his lips tasting their way down over her neck, her shoulders to finally take a rosy-tipped nipple into his mouth. Sharp, aching pains of awareness shot upward from the pit of her stomach, bringing her hips up to meet the hand gently caressing the beginnings of her thighs and the sensitive area between them.

On and on he went, touching, caressing, and squeezing, his hands never still, his lips moving with dedicated purpose to each spot his hands had been. Jo writhed beneath the erotic assault, not knowing from one minute to the next whether or not she could stand it. She heard herself begging him to take her, felt him soothe her pleadings with ways and methods unbelievably stimulating yet delay that final release, that cataclysmic splendor she was seeking.

Finally, when she could no longer stand the aching pain of need, Jo grasped Chase's shoulders and pulled him to her, her arms wrapping themselves around him, binding him to her forever. His thighs covered her parted ones, and she cried out when he claimed her.

Jo pushed herself upward, an uncontrollable urge exploding within her to become part of him. Their bodies became damp with perspiration as months of need and longing became gratified. The rhythm increased, his arms holding her, shielding her through one continuous journey of bursting light to the next. They were caught in the light's brilliance and hurled without mercy into the storm of passion their desire had created.

Jo moved her cheek against the hair-covered chest, the wiry growth tickling her nose. She frowned at this intrusion. Her body was warm, her desire sated, and she refused to wake up. She wanted nothing to force her from Chase's arms.

"Why the frown, sweetheart?" Chase chuckled softly in her ear. His heavy leg was resting across both hers. He had one arm beneath her neck, and his other across her stomach, his hand clasping her hip.

"I refuse to wake up," Jo murmured drowsily without opening her eyes.

"Don't you think we should eat?" he teased.

"Mmmm, maybe, but later. Right now I want to finish my dream."

"Which was?"

"You were making love to me."

"That was no dream," Chase said mockingly. "Would you like me to show you how real it is?"

Jo did open her eyes then and grinned at him. "I think I could manage that—even without food."

Chase's hands slipped around to the softness of her inner thighs, his fingers stroking her body with a gentle urgency. Jo arched against the exquisite fire rapidly building inside her, astonished at how quickly he could arouse her. "This is incredible." She gasped when his tongue began a lazy exploration of the excited tip of a breast.

"I know." Chase raised his head and smiled at her. "Can you imagine what it will be like ten years from now? Even twenty?"

"Yes." Jo spluttered as her head began turning from side to side with anticipation. "We'll be exhausted. Completely worn out." The sound of Chase's laughter was the last coherent thing she remembered for quite a while, her world turning into a kaleidoscope offering color and beauty that outshone anything else she'd ever known.

Several hours later Jo emerged from the bathroom, swathed in a huge towel, and saw Chase, a towel slung low around his hips, standing beside a serving cart, lavishly heaping food onto two plates.

"Something new has been added." She grinned perkily at him as she walked up behind him and slipped her arms around his waist.

"Don't start something unless you intend to finish it," he warned in a deep, husky voice.

"I don't have the energy to 'start' anything," Jo confessed, her nose twitching appreciatively at the tempting aromas drifting up from the cart.

Chase placed the plates on the small table in front of the window, then turned and mimicked a comical bow. "Your dinner, madam."

"Finally." Jo sniffed haughtily, sweeping by him with her nose in the air. "For a while there I thought you planned on starving me to death."

She sat down and immediately picked up her fork. But before she could spear a single delectable shrimp and get it into her mouth, she felt Chase's hand on her wrist.

"Again?" She stared incredulously, her eyes twinkling merrily.

"I'll let you rest for a while. Right now I want a commitment from you," he said slowly, his expression watchful.

Jo let the fork slip from her fingers, the soft thud when it hit the table the only sound in the room.

"Now?" she said quietly. "At this precise moment?"

"Now. At this precise moment. Will you marry me?"

"When?"

"Immediately."

"Don't I even get a few minutes to quibble? A girl can't be too careful, you know. And a measly two dozen roses is hardly what I'd call a decent bribe."

"Would you like diamonds and mink?"

"Would you give them to me?"

"Faster than you can blink your eyes."

"And a Mercedes like yours, only I want a baby-blue one."

"It's yours."

"Well . . ." Jo shrugged, struggling to contain her happiness. "I suppose I'll marry you."

"Good. Now"—Chase released her hand—"you may eat. Then we'll make love again." He leered lasciviously at her.

"When is this wedding going to take place?" Jo asked, something in his manner picking at her peace of mind.

"Sunday afternoon."

"Sunday afternoon!" she exclaimed, the shrimp she'd been about to eat falling back onto the plate. "That's impossible."

"Nothing is impossible when you want it badly enough." Chase grinned, enormously pleased with

285

himself. "My mother and your mother are arranging the whole thing. All you have to do is shop for a dress tomorrow. I'll go along to see that you get something 'proper.' Your mother's instructions," he was quick to add before she hit him. "Amelia has already been filled in on the plans. Jake, Bink, Elise, Mary Clare, Mo, and the entire clan of our relatives and friends will assist her in every possible way with the twins while we are on our honeymoon."

Jo sat back in her chair, thoughtfully tapping her nails against the table. "Exactly how long have you been planning this little affair?" she demanded.

"Two weeks."

"What if I'd said no?"

"That too was considered. I'd made alternate plans for an abduction."

"My children might not approve." She used her final thrust, hoping to put at least one dent in his ornery hide.

"Our children, and they approve heartily. I discussed it with them yesterday at lunch while you were at the office. By the way, my lawyer is drawing up adoption papers for the twins. I don't want any loose ends hanging about."

"Will Bink mind?" Jo asked, feeling as if she'd just completed a marathon.

"He adores you, and you know it. He suggested you move in with us months ago."

"I'll remember to hug him extra hard when I see him."

"Do that." Chase looked at the untouched food on her plate. "Aren't you hungry?"

"No"—she shrugged—"but rather than let good food go to waste, I'll eat it."

"I love you, princess. I promise never to deliberately hurt you," Chase said suddenly, his voice very quiet, very serious.

Jo felt the prickly sensation of tears in her eyes as she stared at him. He meant it, and she believed him. "I know, and I love you."

Chase reached across the table and squeezed her hand, his gaze touching on each feature of her face. She was the dearest thing in the world to him, and he intended spending the rest of his life proving that very fact to her.

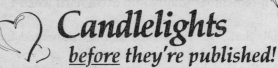